SALVATION

By

Angela Peete

Foreword

Thank you, God, for entrusting me with this gift to write. I will always use it for your Glory. Thank you, Mommy, for believing in me and always pushing me to greater, where I get my creative gene from, I know you are still protecting and guiding me. Thank you to my brothers Eric (Janice) and sisters Janice, Kim, my family, Sharon, Davon, Eric, Aaron, Crystal, Shanita, Keaira and my homies Valda, Nicole, Keena, Vanessa, Bernita, Micailyn, Chelsea and Jessica for always having my back and supporting me. Continue to R.I.P. Mr. Ivan & Tonya Harlee ...and finally, to my Pastor Bishop John D Sheard and Lady Karen Sheard for always continuously praying for me, teaching me and being thee best role models.

Love you Angie Peete

Contents

INTRODUCTION

Rocki swayed to the beat of the angelic choir that stood before her. She felt as if the melodious voice of Pastor J was hypnotizing as he beckoned her to come forward; she stood as applause broke out all around. She imagined her walk as if she finally was getting the Emmy she yearned for in her youth, as she walked forward, she heard her name being yelled; but not Rocki but the name she left behind as if shedding all the pain and stigma Michelle carried, was this what it meant to have your name changed in glory? She heard the pop and turned and faced her past in the form of a bullet as it came barreling towards her, had salvation finally come?

CHAPTER ONE
Born into sin

" Michelle, Michelle! Look at what you are doing, dripping ice cream all over your dress. Lanie come get this girl, she off in her head again," Grandma E roared. "Girl, you on your way to Hollywood, as long as you stay in that imaginary land of yours", tapping Michelle's head, "I don't even know why your daddy and I use that term loosely, would even give you ice cream this early, now we going to be late for church cause you 'dun created another movie in your head". She stormed off laughing to herself, but Michelle did not see the humor, and probably wouldn't for a long time after today. The movie she had created in her mind was nowhere near fiction and soon everyone would know. She heard her mother Lanie scream, before it even came out of her mouth, just as she played it in her mind, "Michelle!" Michelle turns awaiting her fate. Lanie walked up saying, "Girl ain't no time to change now, you either going in that or not at all, go to the bathroom and clean that up", Michelle shook her head in disbelief and ran, but not to the bathroom, but to her room where the "murder" occurred. There was nothing and no one, wait, did she imagine that terribleness? Did it happen at all? She placed her hand down there on the front of her dress and felt the throbbing there was no imagining that, the confusion and embarrassment this pain brought. What, how, why, coursed through her blood as she felt nnumb and in disbelief. She was young enough to be naïve to what just happened but old enough to understand it wasn't right. She remembered Grandma E always talking about the skeezers with the short dresses tempting men was her dress too short. Was it her fault? What is she supposed to do now? would this throbbing never cease a constant reminder of the shame ...

CHAPTER TWO

Shaped in Iniquity.

Rocky! Rocky! Rocky!" The crowd chanted, as Michelle received blow after blow from Trisha. Michelle squinted and looked up at her opponent Trish as she stood over her looking around as if she was Mike Tyson about to completely destroy his opponent, Michelle wanted to yell "It's me, Michelle it's a mistake, what did I do to deserve this?

Michelle has always made it her point to fade in, keep her head down, and not be noticed, she navigated her whole life in this manner until the last month in her 11th-grade year and now here she was after numerous bullying incidents, unprovoked by her she was now at the culmination of it, on the ground between Trish as the crowd called her until the blows hit, then it was "Rocky." The smirk Trish wore on her face was just as humiliating as the blows she dealt Michelle, Trish was looking off in the distance, nodded her head as if she was taking direction, and comprehended the directive, Michelle looked over to see who was the commander and looked into just a pair of eyes, surrounded by a hooded jacket; who was that? but, she didn't have time to think as survival was foremost as the brutal beating commenced.

"Get off her!", an Angel exclaimed in the form of a male voice, The crowd parted immediately, A hand reached out to help Michelle up, "I thought that was you,"This girl don't bother nobody, pick on somebody else, As a matter of fact get off my corner before I hurt every last one of y'all, this better be the last time somebody touch her." The angel roared.

"Thank you so much," Michelle groveled.

"Naw you cool, I'm sorry, my name is Mario, but everybody calls me Cutty." Michelle opened her eyes wide at that name and backed away. Cutty touched her hand again and said, "I see you heard of me. It's okay I'm not a bad guy unless I need to be, come on you need to sit down ; let's go sit on the bus seat."

Michelle wobbled over to the bus seat. She couldn't believe it, not only was she with the most notoriously dangerous drug dealer ever in her city, but he was also the most gorgeous. He was now my guardian angel, Michelle nervously thought, she sat on the edge of the bus seat chair wondering if the butterflies she felt were from the butt whipping or this gorgeous piece of meat beside her. Michelle glanced upwards and mouthed, "Thank you, Lord." Mario quipped, "Amen," and then laughed. That laugh that smile his teeth, brought Michelle into him, to his body, his essence, and his soul and just hugged her, Michelle felt like the earth had swallowed her up.

Mario stood up, after what seemed like an eternity, and said, "are you hungry? Let's get you something to eat." He raised his hand as if he was a CEO calling for his Valet and just as quick as his hand went up his car arrived, a black 300, standard drug dealer car for 1985. Michelle was so confused she felt like the ghetto version of Cinderella, where you get beat up and meet your Prince Charming! She closed her eyes as she sank into the comfort of the seat and wondered what fine restaurant her chariot was taking her to. The blaring yellow light of the local Fast-food restaurant jarred her from her perfect daydream. "Oh well," she thought two out of three ain't bad. They grabbed the food and drove off. Mario looked at her and said, "You still live over on Wellspring?" Michelle choked on her drink. "How did he know?" she thought as Mario smiled that charming smile, "you want to know how I know. Girl, you are not hard to notice." Mario looked at her and then said, "You know how beautiful you are, you keep to yourself and most of all, which is rare, the boys ain't got your name in their mouth saying they been with you.Plus , you know how many people get beat up on that corner?" Michelle hung her head in shame. "Sorry, but that is what happened a beat down! Sorry Im sorry, but the thing is; it's not every day I save them. I thought you would get at least one hit in. What did you do to them?" Michelle shook her head in objection, "I don't even know her," she stammered, "They have been picking on me for the last month or so," Mario said more to himself, "it's okay now.Ain't nobody with good sense going to mess with you. Especially since i'll be picking you up from school now." She stammered, "what?"Michelle's mind was racing, everything was happening too fast for

Michelle's mind to keep up. Mario responded as if he didn't even hear her and the matter was settled, "you got any after-school activities going on?" Michelle shook her head and said, "no." "Ok good then..." A knock on the window interrupted the conversation. Mario rolled down the window angrily, "What Chuck?! Don't you see I'm in here with my girl?!" Michelle choked again on her drink. The boy known as Chuck looked in the window and backed off nervously till, he disappeared around the corner. Mario looked at Michelle then back at the now gone Chuck and laughed, "Oh Lord now they going to think I'm a woman beater, let's get you home and cleaned up." "I'm not ready to go home," she shyly interjected. Mario chuckled, "Aww you going to miss me, don't worry I'll see you tomorrow after school. I promise but you need to get home I'm sure your block got the news and your grandma..." Michelle was shocked he even knew that she existed, let alone, her grandma who as Mario put it, "ain't one to play wit."

True enough, as soon as he pulled up on Wellspring, the block, more specifically her porch was lit up. Grandma E was on the porch along with her mom and people were standing on the steps, the lawn looked as if Grandma E was giving the Sermon on the Mount. Everyone turned when Mario pulled up. The crowd separated as Mario ushered Michelle to Grandma E. Grandma E took one look at my face and then at Mario. "Lanie," yelling to my mom, "go get my purse. People started to leave as if they understood exactly what they may have meant. "Did you hurt my grandbaby? what happened? Why you ain't talking?" She barreled all those questions to Mario.

"Lanie?! Get up and get my purse. Mario backed up,"

"Ms. Elaine, I promise you I had nothing to do with it she was on my str- I mean in my neighborhood and I saw some girl jump her and I stopped them, tell her Michelle," Michelle, who now had a shaky voice as she spoke to her grandmother said, "It's true Grandma E, Mario helped me," Grandma E straightened up, "I'm sorry, let's get you in the house." Michelle took one more glance back as Mario got back in the car and mouthed, "See you tomorrow," Michelle managed a small smile and wave and walked in as Grandma E yelled back at Michelle's mom… "Lanie?!"

Lanie was too much in her own stupor, Michelle mused. Her mom hadn't been the same since her dad left. That is the day she wished she could erase from her memory. Michelle hated ice cream to this very day because of that day which started like any other Sunday: Church with Grandma E, back home for dinner, then back off to church. Michelle never disliked going to church, she loved the stories the preacher, Pastor Sttubs told about God, and the way the choir sang made her feel like she could do anything. But this Sunday was different from the beginning, Michelle's mother didn't wake her up in time because she had a hangover from going to the club with Michelle's father Mr. Des everyone called him. So because of that Michelle didn't have to go to morning service, "but she better be ready for the 11:00 am Service! " Grandma E exclaimed before she left out the door, just as Michelle was waking up.

Michelle was torn between sadness and excitement that she was not going to church but she wanted to see what went on while she was gone. Santori, her sister by a few months was still asleep. Michelle often wondered why Santori never had to go to church, She never even stopped to wonder why she and Santori were only two months apart with the same momma and "daddy". Michelle went to the kitchen and made a piece of toast to eat until her mother woke up to make a big breakfast. Mr. Des turned to her after closing the door and said, "I guess it's just me and my pretty thing." Michelle looked at him and felt the same creepiness he always made her feel whenever she was around him she suddenly lost her taste for her toast. She sat and watched Tv until it was almost eleven and there was no sign of her mom. She retreated to the bathroom, brushed her teeth, and washed her face. Then went into her room, which she shared with Santoria, she was careful not to wake her. Just as she was picking out her new dress, Mr.Des walked in, he placed his finger over his mouth, and scooped up Michelle making her kick over the pencil that was on the desk between her and Santoria's beds. Mr Des looked over to Santori who was still asleep, picked up the pencils, and after placing them back on the desk, laid down on the bed beside Michelle. He placed his hand on Michelle's throat and whispered, "You are my special girl," Michelle squirmed to get away and his hand tightened around her throat and he said, "Be quiet or I'll hurt you, if you are still it won't hurt."

Mr. Des took his time as he outlined her body with his hand and then touched her down there in the spot Grandma E told her No one and she meant no one was to touch. Just as she was about to scream from the pressure his fingers were causing down there he placed his hand on her mouth, Michelle thrashed to no avail with her squirming. Mr. Des' hand was covering her mouth and nose and she felt herself disappearing, at least that is the only feeling she could equate it to. She looked over to focus on anything and looked straight into Santori's eyes which were watching under her pillow. Michelle tried to scream which threw off Mr. Des and he loosened just enough for Michelle to reach out and grab the pencil and jab it straight into His eye. Mr. Des screamed out and released Michele. He fell on the floor, Michelle didn't look back as she grabbed her dress and ran into the bathroom. Michele was so confused; this was her daddy. She felt stupid, what did she do that made her daddy look at her like that? She rubbed her belly, what if she had a baby in her tummy now, and her daddy, who would be the baby daddy ,was now dead, killed by her? She started crying and disappeared under the water to another place where everything was normal, no confusion like what was going on in her head just peaceful all around. Michelle wished she could have stayed in that place but her lungs disagreed and she came up gasping for air. She jumped out of the tub and just as she was getting dressed someone knocked on the door. For some strange reason, her heart started beating rapidly, but as the door opened it was Santori with an ice cream cone. She hugged Michelle and walked out. Michelle walked out and sat in the living room determined not to go back to the murder scene. Grandma E walked in as she was sitting there looking at a blank TV with the now melted Ice Cream in her hand. "Michelle?! Michelle," Who would give you ice cream, probably your daddy and I use that term loosely, now we are going to be late for evening church cause you dun created another movie in your head, after noticing Michelle was just staring off into space. She stormed off but was laughing and muttering, but Michelle didn't see the humor, and probably wouldn't for a long time after today. The movie she had created in her mind was nowhere near fiction and soon everyone would know. She heard her mother Lanie scream before it even came out of her mouth, just as she played it in her mind, "Michelle!" she turned awaiting her fate. Lanie walked up, "Girl ain't no time to change now you either going in that or not at all, go to the bathroom and clean that up", Michelle shook her head in disbelief and ran not to the bathroom but to her room where the "murder" occurred. Where was Daddy? where was Santori? Nothing, no one. Michelle shook her head as if would put the pieces together, did it happen? She rubbed her hand over the lower part of her dress where his fingers had left her forbidden parts as Grandma E called them; throbbing. Michelle changed out her clothes still wondering where they were and what happened after she went to the bathroom. Maybe she had gone to a world like the one she had left in the shower, Here was the world with pain and hurt. . She shook it from her mind but it kept returning as she sat in church, as she went to school the next day, even two days after he disappeared. The only one who suffered because of it was her mom who became quieter and quieter each day until she was just a shell. It felt as if it was just Michelle and Grandma E. Michelle didn't know how to help her and after she came home drunker and drunker as the days grew and blurted out, "He even treated you like you was his own daughter," She stopped trying to help her. Michelle's focus was only on school and Grandma E.

Lanie walked into the room where Grandma E was administering medical assistance to Michelle. "Girl," she amusingly stated, "trouble always seems to find you. What did you do this time?"

"Lanie!" Grandma E exclaimed, "Why would you say that?" Knowing exactly what Lanie was referring to, Michelle got up and ran into the bathroom turned on the water to escape to THERE like she did every time since that fateful day. Michelle thought about the fight this time when Trish was standing over her Michelle kicked out and knocked her down and started kicking her and now everyone was yelling Rocky! Rocky but this time they were talking about Michelle, then she thought of Mario and how if she would've done that her Prince Charming wouldn't have shown up, although she was bruised she liked the second outcome better, the only thing missing was her kiss from Prince Charming, there was always tomorrow. Her world was starting to get cold, so she decided to come back to earth and got out of the now-cold tub.

Grandma E and Lanie were still in the room but arguing now.

"Why do you hate that child so much? You've been like that towards her since Des left." Michelle looked at her mom, Lanie glanced nervously at Michelle, attempted again, and put her head down again after another glance, not as you glance in recognition of someone, but it gave Michelle a glance into her mother's soul and knew that her mother knew. Michelle vocalized it, "You knew" Michelle stammered softly at first then louder with each breath, "You knew, you knew!"

Lanie got wide-eyed, "NO, no, no! Michele, he was sorry, he was drunk and he thought it was me."

Grandma E was bewildered at first, but when Lanie exclaimed that Mr. Des thought Michelle was Lanie; it hit her like a ton of bricks, and then Grandma E hit Lanie like a ton of bricks. "You let that devil hurt my baby, and then treated her like crap all these years, Lanie how could you want someone that bad to share your bed that you let him do that!!!"

Lanie just kept shaking her head and saying, "No, he didn't know, he didn't know."

Grandma E screamed, "Get out, get out of my house now!" Lanie looked up at Michelle and ran out, Grandma E grabbed Michelle in a hug and started praying over her, each word of her prayer released the pain she was holding in all those years and new pain at realizing her mother knew all along. She just cried until she could only heave with no sound, Grandma E tucked her in, and as she was turning off the light Grandma E said, "You don't have to go to school tomorrow." Michele jumped up saying, "No, Mario is bringing me home!" Michelle stammered. I can't miss my kiss, she thought. her mind raced. Grandma E came to the bed and said, "Although, I am so happy he was there for you today, he bad news Baby girl, don't get hooked on him. You stay a few days off until we figure out who is harassing you."

"But, Grandma E,"

"NO butts about it, you only got a few weeks left, and with your grades it'll be okay, you'll go back next week, okay?.I'll call the school tomorrow." And with that she was gone, Michelle went to sleep, and tossed and turned all night. Her dreams ranged from her being punched by Mr. Des "down there" to her mom offering her ice cream to a kiss from Mario and then those eyes! She jumped up, those eyes, where had she seen them? She willed herself to go back to sleep but it was useless. She was scared to see what awaited her. She got out a to-do list.

a.she wrote, kiss Mario b. ... the end. Michelle never felt such a longing for someone so quickly, it must be because he was her Hero, "that's it," she thought, "it will pass." She closed her eyes and instantly Mario's lips came into view. Lord, it wasn't going to go away until she kissed those lips, she surmised.

After breakfast Michelle made the very bad decision to sit on the porch, people came by to offer their "condolences" or that's what it seemed like after countless, "Michelle I heard what happened," or "Wish I was there," or the more popular "couldn't've been me." Michele decided to go back in the house and as she stood to stretch, she saw it, the 300 came down the street slowly, she tried to pretend she didn't see it at first but then he beeped the horn. Michelle smiled and waved to acknowledge she saw him. Michelle walked to the gate as Mario pulled up. He got out of the car with "flowers!" Michelle exclaimed, Mario, smiled and handed her a gift.

They walked up and sat on the porch. Michelle felt all eyes around the neighborhood on her and when she heard her Grandma's phone ringing she knew Ms. Pearl, the nosey neighbor was alerting her to Mario's presence, and she hurried to open the gift.

"Oh, Mario you didn't have to," her excitement wavered at the gift...an ice pack ?! Mario laughed such a beautiful laugh; she forgave his gag gift.

"I'm sorry," he stated between laughs, "I couldn't help it." HEE hee she smirked and reached over to finally get her kiss, when Grandma E creaked open the door, "you alright out here Michelle?"

"Yes Grandma E, you remember Mario from yesterday? He came by to check on me and brought me flowers."

"Hmmm hmmm," Grandma E exclaimed, "that's nice, don't be out here long you need your rest and with that, she turned and went back in the house.

"Your grandma be on it, she don't play" Mario quipped. Michelle went to defend her and said, "She just," But Mario cut her off mid-sentence, "She just loves you, I know that's cool. I ain't never had that in a while, but I," looking at Michelle with meaning, "think I'm going to be alright now". Michelle vowed at that moment to make sure she was the only one who he received it from. She leaned over to kiss him and the glare of the siren made them both jump apart, Mario laughed "Is God trying to tell us something?"

"Time to tell your friend see you later!" Grandma E barked from the kitchen.

"See you later Grandma E, see if you can leave the porch tomorrow I'm a come get you early tomorrow." Mario quipped

Michelle jumped in anticipation, "Where are we going?" Mario laughed as he opened the car door. "Get off the porch tomorrow and you'll see." With that, he drove off into the sunset.

Tomorrow couldn't come fast enough, Michelle got up extra early, cleaned up, and went and checked on Grandma E while she was still in bed watching her stories before cooking.

"I'll be back around 1 Grandma E, see you" and ran out before she could ask any questions. Michelle purposefully left her phone there in case she tried to call after she saw her pull off with Mario. No need for a phone; being with Mario made her whole day and she didn't have any friends anyway. It seemed like they drove for hours not saying anything, a kiss on the hand here and there. Michelle was content with just the ride, Mario already made Michelle feel it was all about her. every time his phone rang he ignored it until he finally turned the phone off. After what seemed like a beautiful eternity they turned into a beautiful house in the middle of nowhere. Michelle's nerves surfaced, was this the Kingpin's house? Was she about to be in the middle of a shoot-out?

"Calm down" Mario's laugh interrupted her thoughts, "girl, your body tightened up so hard," he laughed again. "Girl I ain't let nothing happen to you before and I wouldn't let you nothing happen to you. Haven't I already proved that?"

"I know, I trust you," Michelle's body relaxed as she spoke. Mario navigated the car up the long beautifully manicured lawn. It felt like a scene in a movie. "Where are we? This is so beautiful, what do they even call this place?" Michelle questioned.

"Home sweet home," Mario spoke in retrospection.

"What?" Michelle gasped as they finally pulled up to the front door, "do you live here with your parents?" She asked, Straightening herself to look more presentable.

"Kind of, sort of,"

"But-" she prodded.

"Shh no more questions until after we eat," Mario interrupted. They exited the car and entered through the garage into one of the most expansive living rooms Michelle had ever entered in reality. Her dreams still had not prepared her for this beauty. "Oh Mario this is absolutely beautiful"

"I actually did all this myself,"

"Not bad for a thug from the hood."

"Come on let me take you on a brief tour before the food gets cold." Mario took her all over from the bedrooms to the bowling alley, indoor pool, it was, like, heaven on earth. Michelle felt like she had walked through a whole mall by the time they reentered the Living room.

"Will your parents be home soon?" Michelle inquired.

"They're right here, Mom, Dad, I would like to introduce you to someone," Mario turned Michelle around to face the fireplace in the Living room, where two beautiful vases sat on the mantelpiece. Michelle turned around to Mario, "Oh Mario I'm sorry. What happened?" Mario grabbed her hand and led her away to the kitchen. "No more questions until after we eat, okay?"

Dinner was two take-out orders of seared lamb, mashed potatoes, and grilled asparagus from the local strip club, bourgeois on a budget. They ate in silence and nodded to how good the food was. Michelle savored each bit of the deliciousness of the lamb until Mario interjected her thoughts, "Girl you eat like a bird," Michelle didn't want to tell him that she was only eating slowly because there weren't any seconds. She was saddened as she took the last bite because it punctured her dreams and brought her back to the reality that the date was almost ending.

"Would you like dessert?" Mario asked, as if reading her thoughts. How was it, in the little days that she and Mario knew each other, she knew he would be her only pilot to cloud nine.

"Of course," Michelle replied.

"Ok I'll put it in the oven and we can go into the living room and talk until it's ready, okay?"

Michelle nodded her head in agreement.

As they made their way back to the living room, Michelle couldn't help but still be in awe, as if seeing this path for the first time. Mario stopped short, "Want to go on another tour? We can talk as we walk." Wow, there's more, "Ok," Michelle agreed.

"My parents were the late great and still present. Mr. and Mrs. Mario and Tekesha Richardson. I am their only child I grew up an army brat until my mom finally passed the bar and my dad retired from the Army and became a State Trooper. One night literally the ending to my 16th birthday and the night of my parents' Anniversary we were leaving the restaurant and two people pulled up on the side of us and kept gesturing for us to roll the window down but they waving a gun, my dad told my mom to keep on driving but they were cut off and my mom was dragged out the car, my dad jumped out telling them to get off of her. I remember hearing my mom scream once and I just sat there and watched her slump as if she fainted. My dad ran back towards the car, the man must've thought he had a gun in the car and the man with the gun just started shooting wildly. My dad was shot In the back of his head and my mom died of a heart attack. My mom's brother gained custody of me and treated me as if I was his slave until he found out my trust fund could not be touched until I turned 18. So he bounced and no one ever checked up on me until I was 18 then the courts came in and turned everything over to me. Soooo, now I'm like a superhero going around saving women on the street. I hope you don't think you were the first person," he mocked laughing. Michelle jokingly grabbed her chest, "what?" she joked, I'm not the first?" Mario looked into her eyes, kissed her, and said, "No, but you will be my last," Michelle's mind began to race, she wasn't ready, she had pictured her first time as someone's wife but in Mario's arms she felt there was no need to wait. She shook her head to erase the doubt; whatever tomorrow brings she was ready for tonight. An alarm rang in her mind which brought her back to the reality of the smoke detector going off.

They ran to the kitchen where the smell of charred peaches was in the air. Mario took off his shirt to fan the smoke away from the smoke detector. "Yes." Michelle thought as she looked as his naked back, she was ready... Mario interrupted her thoughts, tonight's destiny, and the promise of tonight, "oh well," Mario interjected, "just ice cream it is." Michelle's mind spiraled, she was now in Grandma E's kitchen with the ice cream dripping down her hands and that throbbing down there like the erratic beating of a tribal war drum, she locked her hands tight to suppress the bile and vomit threatening to come up every time someone mentioned or she saw ice cream.

They say your past flashes before your eyes before you die and Michelle wished for death because that would be better than the laughing, she was sure Mario was doing right now, if only she could will herself to open her eyes. But this time her body was in complete control over her mind; and that's when she felt a hand on her back, she flinched and tried to run from her daddy but he had her pinned down again. Then he whispered in her ear "come back Michelle, I got you, its ok."

The image she had in her mind dwindled as she now placed the voice with Mario who was hugging her and rubbing her back and whispering in her ear "'Its ok what's wrong? stop crying, please talk to me Michelle." Mario coaxed. Michelle gently pushed him back and wiped her tears to let him know she was ok.

"I'm sorry but you know how certain smells make you think of a favorite memory? Mine is opposite, Ice cream brings up bad childhood memories. I'm so sorry and embarrassed." Michelle went to walk in the living room to explain further. "Its ok, we all have crosses to bear, maybe its time I took you home anyway its a long drive back to your house and I don't want your grandma mad at me." Mario explained. Michelle looked in his eyes for reassurance that he wasn't trying to get rid of her for good but he was already putting on his shirt and collecting his stuff to leave. Maybe she wasn't ready after all.

The ride home was a series of jazz music and quietness. The only hope Mario offered was to grab her hand and kiss it ever so often. MIchelle gave herself a pep talk the whole way home to ask him, beg him not to let that episode scare him away. Before she could even speak as they pulled up to the house, Mario spoke, "Michelle I have to go out of town to take care of some business Ill be back this weekend. Wait a minute, ask Grandma E if she will come over my house and I can sit and talk to her and she get to know me and not what she heard or thinks about me. Family is very important to me and I don't want her thinking bad about me at all."

Michelle hesitated, remembering Grandma E's words, "that boy gonna be the death of you, he trouble, Chelle." As if Grandma E could smell Michelle, the front light came on.

"I'll see and let you know, text me when you make it home." Michelle boldly reached over and kissed Mario on his lips and rushed into the house before Grandma E could come on the porch. Michelle knew the impossibility of slipping past Grandma E, so she walked in and braced herself. "Grandma E, I'm home "trying to sound as nonchalant as possible. Grandma E softly said " come join me for tea in the kitchen Chelle. Two things Michelle hated were soft speaking from Grandma E and drinking tea with Grandma E. She walked into the kitchen and sat at the table while Grandma E poured the already boiling water. Michelle knew she was ready to pounce, she knew she had to defend this relationship with Mario; her decision to be with him, and stand her ground for Grandma E to understand that she was in it for life.

Grandma E as usual started the convo "Because that boy was there for you when you most needed help, I'll never force you to stop seeing that boy,"

Michelle relaxed. Grandma E then led her assault by saying, "But just answer me one question."

"Yes ,Grandma E?," Michelle relented,

"Are you just seeing him out of gratitude? What do you know about him? Do you know every one saying he a drug dealer? Are y'all having sex? Does he go to church?!"

Grandma E came with a barrage of questions. "I will answer all your questions, or better yet you can ask him yourself he wants to take all of us out to talk to you."

"Talk to me about what?! " responded Grandma E.

"I cant with you Grandma E, but I really like Mario he is not what they say about him. He is very good to me, for me. He pushes me and he never tries to get me to leave school, as a matter fact he makes sure I don't leave."

"Sound like he hiding something," Grandma E interjected.

"No he just understand the importance of pursuing your dreams." Michelle defended.

"Im sorry," Grandma E consoled Michelle, "its just after that beat down last year"...

"Wait beat down it wasn't exactly a beat down." Michelle interrupted.

Grandma E laughed and said, "I may have been in a church all my life but I know a beat down when I see one, did you even fight back?"

Michelle put her head down.

"I'm sorry baby ain't nothing wrong with being sensitive but you have to learn how to take care and protect yourself and I ain't gonna always be around to kiss your boo boo, or worse you have to be able to survive enough to make it home. I am going to reserve judgement on Mario until we talk, but learn karate, take a boxing class, something that wont have me worried every time you leave me. Have you even found out why or seen those girls?"

" No, I haven't even seen the girl that had the problem with me its like they all disappeared and no one bothers me since they find out I'm Mario's girl. It's li- ;"

"Mario girl? Ain't no label until he talk to me Big Momma E." They both burst out laughing.

"Girl I'm going to bed and you better too, school ain't over yet. Have you made a decision about what school you going to?"

"I haven't made a decision yet" Michelle hemmed. Grandma E instincts kicked in, "you better be making this decision based on you not your boyfriend, and especially not me, I'm a be fine I lived my life you go live yours and then you'll come back here and well live here all together with our cats, and if you marry Mario then one dog."

She bust out laughing at her own joke as she put her dishes that she washed away. "So when does Mr. Mario want to meet?" Grandma E asked.

"Ill ask him is this Sunday ok?" Michelle responded. Grandma E winked slyly at Michelle and said, "perfect we can go to church and then have dinner here and we can talk, ok?" Michelle, looking like a deer in headlights at the thought of asking him to go to church.

"Yes ma'am" Michelle squeaked out. "What's wrong Michelle, you scared to ask him to go to church? that says something right there," laughed Grandma E as she kissed Michelle on the cheek and walked inside and if Michelle guessed right danced a little jig as she twirled to close her bedroom door as if the matter was non-negotiable and settled.

Michelle took her now lukewarm tea to her room and dialed Marion, then hung up then redialed then hung up. Then decided it was too late, she coaxed herself to tell herself that it was better if she called him in the morning when she was more awake and braver. The phone rang in opposition just as she was about get in the bed. She instantly knew it was Mario because the only two people that called her were Grandma E and Mario.

"Hello?" she stammered,

"Hey I was in the shower, I see you called me a couple times, everything ok?" Mario asked.

"Yes," Michelle continued to stammer, "I talked to Grandma E about you coming to talk to her and she said this Sunday, aaand she wants you go to church with us and then have dinner here." Michelle blurted out.

Mario responded without hesitation, "ok cool."

Michelle was surprised and said as much, "you will? I thought you wouldn't want to."

Mario laughed I won't hold it against you this time because we are getting to know each other, but it's always best to communicate and ask if you want answers. And I will do the same with you, ok?"

Michelle responded, "ok, you right I'm sorry Mario,"

"See you Sunday you gotta go to bed so you can get up on time for school. Good night" said Mario as he hung up the phone

"+"

Sunday couldn't come fast enough for Michelle. She fantasized about her and Mario 'mistakenly" wearing the same outfit to church. It would definitely let everyone know that they were together. She walked down the halls of school at a fast pace as if that would quicken time until Sunday. Saturday came and Michelle picked out a black Adidas dress, she thought about calling him but it was like a test of their "new love." She knew enough of him to know he loved black.

Sunday boasted the cloudiest day, "bad omen," Michelle thought then shook that thought from her head. Grandma E would love Mario once she got to know him. Then she faced something she kept ignoring as it gnawed at her. She really didn't know much past his parents dying, him being rich, and him helping her from being, in Grandma E's words, "beat down."

He seemed eager to meet Grandma E, too eager she sometimes felt. Nerves were running ragged as she went to the kitchen to make something that wouldn't come back up because of the butterflies that now resided in her stomach.

The ringing of the doorbell did nothing but bring on a near panic attack. Grandma E rushed past Michelle as if she was the girlfriend, This did give Michelle time to calm her nerves. In walked Mario with a custom-made blue suit that will have the Pastor dealing with the spirit of envy. Michelle was devastated, he failed the first test. She felt so underdressed, she realized she misunderstood him once again and should've just asked.

Michelle whispered, "I'll be right back." she ran a put on the first frillier blue dress she could find, she wanted to look dainty and feminine beside Mario today as if it was their wedding day. Grandma E yelled, "Come on girl or we leaving you." Michelle was shocked by Grandma E's one hundred-eighty-degree turnaround about Mario and had Michelle barely tweak out, "coming," forgetting she was trying on two different shoes to see which one went better.

"Michelle! Grandma E screeched, YOU ARE NOT Going to church making any new fashion statement." Mario pointed down to her shoes. "Oh no," she gasped and ran back to her bedroom and changed into the matching shoe, and ran back out.

The car ride was... fast "Grandma E why are you going so fast? We are going to be super early at the rate you going." Grandma E was so focused on driving that Michelle didn't think she heard her until Grandma E said, "We have to get a good seat. Everyone going flip when I walk in, I'll be at the top of the board in no time,"

Michelle knew there was more to it when she agreed so quickly. She thought she brought the top sinner to "find the Lord" today. She looked at Mario to apologize for Grandma E making him uncomfortable but he was just sitting there with the widest smile, enjoying every moment of the ride. I really don't know him at all! thought Michelle. But Michelle promised after today she was going to make sure she found out everything about him

Church was beautiful, although Mario didn't join when they extended the right hand no matter how hard Grandma E pushed. He did stand and thank her for inviting him and told everyone he would be back next Sunday. A ting of jealousy surged through Michelle as everyone around her applauded. She didn't want to share Mario with anyone. When Mario sat down Grandma E gave him the biggest hug and Michelle was ready to go.

They left the church after what seemed like hours and hours after Grandma E paraded Mario around to everyone, especially Hazel, not once glancing back at her true granddaughter, Michelle thought. Oh well she thought suck it up because Grandma E could hate him.

Dinner was a glorious combination of Thanksgiving, Christmas, and Cinco de Mayo! Grandma E went all out. Michelle was confused, was she showing out to let Mario know that his "drug dealing" money was no good or to really welcome him and get to know him? The way she was fawning all over Mario she began to see it was the latter. Mario gulped down the meal in between questions. That is until Grandma E started to get to the marrow of the matter.

"You seem to have so much potential Mario, why you selling them drugs?" Grandma E said without hesitation.

Michelle wanted to interrupt but both Grandma E and Mario both stopped her.

"It's ok, I can answer any question she has about me better than anyone can answer for me. I have never once sold what you call them drugs. I was left an inheritance by my parents, you ever heard of the Richardson Law firm?" Grandma E nodded her head in recollection.

"That was my mom's firm until her passing," Mario continued. "My mom died of a heart attack and my dad was killed, both were on my 16th birthday. I've basically been on my own ever since. Because I didn't receive my inheritance until I turned 18. I had to learn how to survive on the streets and met a lot of cool cats— sorry no disrespect Grandma E."

She prodded him to continue, looking at Grandma E, the first thing that came to mind was "mesmerized," Michelle thought. A lot of my mom's business associates gave me info to start my own business in trading so I went to school and have been doing that ever since, but I still stay in contact with my friends and that's when the rumors started "how can this young man who didn't have a pot to —- you know what they said," Grandma E hung her head knowing she had participated in some of that gossip. "How this boy get all that money in two years? He gotta be up to no good". When actuality I just was a product of my new environment. I just learned how to not get consumed by it. I was honestly fine with how I was until I met Michelle and realized I wanted more. Then to see how you care for her, the kind of caring I missed from family. Even if it doesn't work out between Michelle and myself...,"

Michelle's heart began thumping so hard at the thought, while Mario continued, "I hope we can all still be family." Grandma E grabbed Mario up in a hug and said, "Son you will always be family." Michelle knew it was nothing she could do about the bond that just formed and she was ok with it.

CHAPTER THREE

"Am i being paranoid?"

Days turned into months, months into years and now Michelle who was a Senior in college and was home on winter break to see her man, Mario, and Grandma E. Mario had become Grandma E's partner in crime, if you could commit crimes in church. They were inseparable. He was at every revival, convention, and Bible Study. He even started telling Michelle she needed to get herself back in a relationship with "da Lord". Michelle didn't mind because Mario finally had what he had been searching for a family and she had a friend. Although, Mario and Michelle were more than just friends, their relationship was nothing more than friends, especially since Mario decided, after a "revelation" from Bible Study, that it was better to wait. The church had a guest Speaker on that night and he said that so many young people rush to sex; as if that seals the deal, as if it is proof of their love. "Sex is not the climax or culmination of a relationship, but the beginning of a lifelong vow made after marriage of the person's commitment to one another" he stated.

Mario felt it was for him, and that he and Michelle should wait until they were married to express that commitment and for her to resolve anything that would hinder their wedding night and future. But Mario still made sure she knew that the wedding was the result for them, and Michelle decided it was worth the wait.

Michelle decided to meet up with Mario for lunch after she got a rest from traveling. Grandma E went on a shopping mall run and lunch with her church gals.

Michelle woke from her nap and decided it was time to work on the "things" that Mario spoke of that might hinder her future, and Michelle did something she hadn't done in a long time and that was to call her mother. As the phone rang, Michelle's heart was beating like a rabbit in an open desert, scared it may become the next meal or snack. She tried to calm her nerves.

"The ball is in my court," she thought, "I called her, so I can direct the conversation any way I want." The "Hello" from Lanie made Michelle feel like the awkward teen again.

"Hey Mom" Michelle stammered, "I was just calling to see how you were doing. And to see if we could talk."

Lanie's voice smiled, "Oh Michelle it's so good to hear from you, I thought it was best just to stay away but I miss you every day. I just want to say I'm sorry I wasn't there when…"

"It's okay "Michelle interrupted, not wanting to tread the path of the past ,yet. I'm in town can I see you today or whenever you can come this weekend? Lanie enthusiastically replied, "of course I will be there,But tell my Momma, so she won't be doing all that yelling when she sees me. Ok?" Lanie inserted. Ok see you then, Michelle said with her heart already feeling light. She hung up happy with the direction the call took. As she lay across the bed she felt so much lighter. While the promise of new beginnings do make situations better, what was that scripture Grandma E told Mario during their home Bible Study: All things work together for the good of them that love the Lord. Now although she wasn't going to church, she did love God. She tried going to one of the churches on campus but she chose the one that had the quickest service time which lasted for just 20 minutes and it was done. And it was also boring. She knew better than to continue there but she didn't make an effort to go to any other one. Sorry Lord, she mentally said to God, she reached over and pulled out the heavily used Bible; by Grandma E, from the nightstand. She decided to read it to seal the deal of her apology. The first scripture she came to read, "Call on me in the day of trouble and I will deliver you". An indescribable eerie feeling came over her and she quickly shut the book. She shook off the feeling that she was going to need that and started to dress up to ignore the gnawing feeling that was creeping up on her.

That feeling stayed with Michelle as she "slept" or tried to and also as she tried to get dressed, she tried to shake that feeling off. As she showered, she imagined this feeling going down the drain right along with the water that ran off her body. By the time she received the call from Mario it was well past lunch time so she took Grandma E's car and met him at his house. Mario left the door open as he always did, "he said it reminded him that he was safe in his home away from everyone." She walked in and Mario hadn't finished dressing. "I thought you would be done and ready to go" Michelle queried. "Lets just stay here and talk I could whip something up or order in", Mario pleaded. Michelle emphatically shook her head no, "we rarely go out, between me being at school and you being at church, we only have time to just grab a bite to eat and by we, I mean you, Grandma E and me".Mario started to interrupt; "how about this, Michelle interjected after looking at her watch, let's go catch a movie and then come back for dinner here, how does that sound?" That sounds good, let's sit down and talk Michelle. Mario said as he led Michelle to the couch.

Michelle was nervous as they sat, that sinking feeling which disappeared when she met up with Mario, now returned. "Is everything ok Mario, if you want, we can just eat here" "No, it's nothing like that, nothing bad." Mario took Michelle's hand. We've been together for almost 5 years now, and I think we should start planning for the next five years. Dont you?" " Yes, Michelle stammered out hoping and praying.Michelle was nervous he was about to ask the most important question in the world. "Where exactly do you see yourself in five years, am I in your plans? Mario asked. "Yes of course! Michelle declared, she grasped Mario's face in her hands, I see us married with 1 kid and one on the way, me working from my pharmaceutical company and you will be walking in from... "Church,Mario interjected, from church after planning my Sermon for Sunday". Michelle must have looked shocked because Mario stated, "come back Michelle don't be shocked" I really feel like God has called me into being a Servant of His, I've never felt this free. I've been chasing ghosts all my life paying people to keep me safe by buying bottles in the club, acting like the biggest drug dealer on the planet and all this time freedom was one name away. Just calling on Jesus brought me the Salvation, freedom, and the peace I always desired. Grandma E saw it in me and confirmed it and I've been in classes with my Pastor. You know how weird and beautiful that sounds , My Pastor. Everything is coming together for me, Michelle all I need is you to complete this. Do you think you can be a Pastor's wife?" but Michelle still stood awestruck by the statement, Mario stood up, "I know it is a lot to take in one moment, can we at least wait until after the movie to come back and discuss it? Unless you say no, leaning towards her, then we can wait for some months and then I can hear that yes". Mario laughed and Michelle shook her head, I promise we will talk about it after the movie.

Michelle wanted to scream, I will follow you until the ends of the earth, but something in her held back. Defeated, she just became quiet. She loved Micheal but did she love him enough for this life altering change. This was not to be taken lightly she was scared to lose herself and in that moment, she felt the weight of the maturity and responsibility to be a leader . She wasn't ready she was sure of it. Because her body shook at the mere thought of having to live that daily.

CHAPTER FOUR
"It ain't my fault"

The ride to the cinema was in total silence, as they were both lost in their thoughts. The movie was a sloppy love story that did nothing but leave Michelle in her own thoughts. Her thoughts took her back. Could she be a Pastor's wife, although she grew up in church it hadn't exactly grown up in her. She knew Mario wasn't talking about right then and there, but she didn't want to lie to him. But then she wasn't ready to lose him anytime soon either. She decided to tell him she was down for it, you never know what or who may change down the road. She felt like it wasn't a need to stir the pot, although the car ride was silent Michelle kept her hand nestled in Mario's to show the unspoken solidarity that she felt towards him. She even started imagining herself standing side by side with her husband Pastor Mario as they looked over their congregation, maybe she could get used to this. Mario interrupted her dream and she noticed they had pulled up to the local food strip mall which had every store from Indian, Chinese, to American. "I know I said I would cook butttt, Mario admitted sheepishly. Michelle couldn't decide if she wanted Chinese or Indian so they decided on a dish from each. They placed their orders and as they were walking back to the car to wait, Michelle jumped and started looking around. She started to get that uneasy feeling again, the Scripture came to her mind again, to call on Jesus while He may be found.

Michelle whispered to the air, "Im losing my mind."

"What? You okay? Did you say something?"

"No," Michelle said shaking off that feeling and hugging Mario to enforce it but she still felt like they were being watched. They got in the car and Michelle needed to talk to get it off her chest and also change whatever feeling she was having.

Michelle started as soon as they got in the car, "Mario, about what we talked about earlier," but Mario interrupted, "no let it wait until Ive had a full belly," he quieted her

"But Mario," Michelle insisted but Mario shushed her, picked up his little bible that he kept in his pocket, and read from it jokingly, "With patience wait for it, See even the Lord is saying to hold up," Michelle laughs and grabs at Bible and said, "let me find my own Scripture," as she reaches for it, Mario grabs it away and tucks it in the pocket of his shirt and said "We can look at it later my dear," and kisses her on lips as he gets out of the car to get food.

Michelle smiled as Mario walked out of one store into the next to get the other food items. She closed her eyes and dreamed of her perfect her world when she opened her eyes and realized they were at the same corner were they met and now here she was, full circle. She thought about how her life was coming together far from how it started. She even was beginning to really thaw on her mom, "oh no!" Michelle exclaimed. She forgot her mom was coming over and just as she reached to call her, her phone was ringing and it was her mom.

Simultaneously, she heard Mario yell out, "Hey, I remember you," and that's when she saw the back hooded figure and heard the gun shots. She dropped her phone and screamed as the figure turned around and she came face to face with her past, the same face that stood on the corner and caused her grief with each blow and she knew her love's death, who was now slumped on the ground, was her fault.

She didn't know what to do, it was total mayhem. People were screaming and Michelle jumped into the driver seat to take off because the hooded enemy was headed towards her car, she closed her eyes and screamed out, "Jesus help me!" and that's when she heard it - the squeal of the siren. She opened her eyes to see the figure disappear around the corner. She jumped out of the car and ran to Mario who was barely holding on.

"Leave now," he muttered, "you're not safe."

Michelle shook her head saying, "no, Mario my answer was going to be yes. I promise I was going to say yes."

Mario tried to smile but started to cough, he grasped Michelle really hard and said, "Go now Ill see you in the morning okay? Go."

Michelle jumped in Mario's car and drove all the way to his house and ran in to get her keys off the kitchen counter. She had no time to think she had to get Grandma E car back. She wanted to spend the night there and just lay in his bed. She felt bad she didn't know his uncle to let him know and questioned whether leaving was the right thing but she thought about it and didn't want to be caught up in anything. She decided to take the car back and take a Taxi back to Mario's house and then leave for school. If it was true that this girl was after her then she would be safe until she left for school.

Michelle sped down the highway to Grandma E. She felt like she was the only one she could tell the only one who could help her sort this out. When Michelle turned on her block she was greeted with the lights of police cars and the yellow tape from the police. Michelle's mind only registered that they were coming to question her about Mario death. It wasn't until she saw her Mother on the front lawn sobbing uncontrollably that she knew it was for something different. She tried to get past the tape but was restrained by the cops. She yelled out to her mom who ran up to her yelling, "she's gone, she's gone. They killed my momma."

Michelle ran to go in the kitchen . When she walked in and saw Grandma E feet pointed lifeless towards the ceiling, Michelle's world became dark all around her...

Michelle woke with a blaring headache, She jumped up realized she was not in her bed but at the hospital. Michelle pressed her hand or tried to press her hand to stop the throbbing in her head but she was handcuffed to the bed and the terrible events of the night came rushing back to Michelle's memory..Mario and Grandma E were gone. Was the girl an ex of Mario? No she thought as she shook her head, the fight happened before she met Mario.. But why Grandma E? Was her mom connected and Mario died because of her and her family's problems? Why was she chained to the bed, did they think she killed them?!

She was at such a lost state she closed her eyes to sleep her thoughts away, and just then her mother walked in with a cop.

"Michelle?" Lanie squeaked, still shaken by the day's events. Michelle could hear the tiredness in her voice.

"Are you awake? Officer Gomez would like to ask you a few questions if you're up for it."

"Michelle Blake ?" Officer Gomez's voice boomed through Michelle , rushing straight to remind her of her returning headache.

"Please, my head hurts," she pleaded. "Ma I need an aspirin, please get me a nurse."

Lanie looked from Michelle to Officer Gomez, caught between wanting to comfort and assist her daughter and also wanting the answers she desperately needed. She chose to help her daughter and get the answers later as she exited the room in search of the nurse on duty. Michelle watched her mom exit then focused on Officer Gomez, she was surprised to say the least when she noticed how young he was and that he was black. She tried to sit up and realized once again she was in handcuffs.

"Why am I handcuffed? Officer Gg..." she stammered.

"It's Officer Gomez,"

"I know,"

He smiled and Michelle's heart beat in a familiar pattern, she looked away guilty she was lusting over some other man moments after losing the love of her life and her beloved Grandma.

"You kept trying to leave and we had questions on both the death of your Grandmother and a Mr Mario (flipping his little notebook) A...Mr Mario, Richardson." Michelle interjected. "So its true," Michelle weakly muttered.

"Im sorry, yes. Im glad you awoke in time for your Grandmother's funeral but Mario was released to his surviving family member."

Michelle stood up and said, "wait, hold up."

She stuttered, "how long have I been asleep?" Not remembering even putting up a fight at all. Last thing she remembered she was walking up the steps to Grandma E…

"Two weeks," Officer Gomez jostled Michelle from her thoughts as he was walking around the opposite side of the bed to take the handcuffs off.

"As I stated," he began, "you are not a suspect, but I am here in an official capacity. I just have a few questions are you ready to talk?"

Michelle shook her head and said, "yes Officer Gomez."

"Connor," Officer Gomez interjected.

Michelle shook her head not understanding,

"Call me Connor." Michelle couldn't help but laugh.

"I know I know a black man with a Irish first name and a Mexican last name." Connor offered as he laughed. Michelle's heart did that weird but familiar pit pat and she focused her gaze on her now released wrist. She vigorously rubbed her wrist as if it would erase the memories in her mind and the guilt she felt for…*never mind* her heart opposed. Officer Connor shook her from her thoughts with his booming voice that was clearly ready for business as he began his barrage of questions.

The next forty five minutes felt like she was on a reality detective show.

"Did you get a good look at the person? What was he wearing? Did they try to harm you? Were drugs involved? Did they tell you they already shot your Grandma?"

Michelle weakly answered no to them all. Officer Gomez peered through her soul, Michelle thought did he think she was lying? She felt like if she said something it would mean the end of her.

"Sorry Grandma E," she muttered.

"I'm sorry I wish I didn't have to ask these questions but the quicker we jump in a lead the safer you'll be."

Lanie and the attending nurse walked in interrupting, she looked at Officer Gomez questionably and he motioned for them to talk outside the door.

He looked at Michelle and said, "Michelle I'll let you rest I'll be here all night so if you remember anything just call out to me."

Michelle shook her head as she ingested the pills the nurse guaranteed would let her rest. She closed her eyes to think about Grandma E and Mario, she felt like everything she wanted and had hoped to achieve was gone now that she had no one to make proud to share in whatever path life produced, she was stuck in a nightmare and was scared to leave because it still held memories of the ones who were no longer there. Michelle watched as Lanie and Officer Gomez chatted outside the door as her eyelids started to droop.

Michelle dreamed she was on the beach. Grandma E was in the seat on her right side telling her she had to remain strong and use wisdom to make her proud, Michelle knew Mario wasn't going to be far from Grandma E. Sure enough, he was standing at the edge of the water telling Grandma E to come look at the water and Grandma went and stood by Mario they both had their back to Michelle explaining how beautiful it was.

Michelle got up to see and Grandma E turned and said, "its not time yet but we love you," as they walked into the water suddenly a big wave came and Mario said, "get up Michelle, hurry up, leave and save yourself. We love you!"

She woke just as they walked away into the wave. Michelle woke to utter darkness and looked out at the glass partition to see if Officer Gomez was there but his chair was empty, "he must've gone to the vending machine," she thought.

She stood up to go relieve herself as she was coming back she took one more look as she sat down on the edge of the bed and he still wasn't back in the chair. Just as she went to lay down a shadow stepped out on the other side of the nurses station that made her skin crawl. She was sure it was the same person although the back was to her she felt it was . The figure appeared to be checking rooms and then not satisfied went into the next room.

Mario's voice rang through her mind, "hurry up and leave." She went to the closet to see if any of her clothes were left in there. Although she was groggy, the adrenaline was now kicking in. She started praying asking God to get her through she peeped out to see the figure stop and look around and went to the next room. Michelle was afraid to breathe as she put on her pants and the outfit she was last in two weeks ago. She peeped out and didn't see the figure anymore and her heart skipped a beat as she realized she may be on her side Michelle looked around and without thinking dashed under the hospital bed with moments to spare. As she just adjusted herself to fit under the bed but still have a view of the door, the figure stealthily opened and walked in, took what sounded like Michelle's chart from the end of the bed, ruffled through the chart, placed it back on the bed, and walked over to the bathroom and slowly opened the door.

Not finding anyone there the figure swore violently and came back to stand by the bed, Michelle was sure her heartbeats were heard. This time her prayers became stronger and more earnest. As she prayed she looked around for anything and saw the dangling cord from the nurse's call, she reached out and pressed the button to summon the nurse. She kept pushing as she begged God to send down an angel to get her through this, she promised to do whatever he wanted if He would get her out of this and He answered by voices in the hallway and the beautiful sound of a police walkie-talkie!

The figure swore again and placed the hoodie back over their head. "Soon, Michelle will get what she deserved, the figure thought" as they raced out the door. While walking out the door and turning left out the door Officer Gomez who was just returning from the restroom, yelled out "Stop!" The figure paused for a moment long enough for Officer Gomez to look in Michelle's room and see her bed empty.

"Michelle?" Officer Gomez attempted to coax who he thought was Michelle back to the room ."Don't leave if you remember something lets talk about it." The figure now satisfied after hearing the police words decided to add icing to the revenge cake turned to face Officer Gomez and shot the gun twice once in his chest and once in his stomach .Deciding the police officer needed to be finished .While walking up on Officer Gomez to exact more pain ,the screams of the nurses made the figure run down the hall to the steps where the "chariot" awaited.

Michelle watched as Officer Gomez yelled her name out to the stranger. Michelle wanted to yell out "That's not me I'm here under the bed hiding to live." She placed her hand over her mouth to stop herself from screaming as the two shots rang out and watched as the figure came back instead of running away.

She caught a glimpse of the cold hard eyes of the figure just as the nurses started screaming and watched as the figure ran off. Michelle scrambled out from under the bed as she heard the nurse yell, "The patient in here just shot the cop!"

"No, I didn't!" Michelle stated, scurrying from under the bed "That wasn't me. I was hiding under the bed." The nurse ran over to help and assist Michelle. Michelle slid down on the floor hopeless as the unit of the hospital came alive with doctors and more police. Michelle felt the walls closing in yet again the only sigh of relief came after many hours of praying, sitting, and more praying, the word came that Officer Gomez was expected to make it. Michelle went to the waiting room to calm herself and get away from the craziness. It seemed as if every cop was in the hospital. Even though she felt safer here than on the street; the plan to get away from all this began to play out in her mind. She looked around and everyone seemed to be caught up in their own world and she decided it was now or never.

Michelle hesitated one final time as her heart's palpitations caused her to decide if she should take the stairs and risk the killer still being in the hospital staircase or the elevator and risk the cops realizing that she was trying to escape and be waiting for her on the main floor. She decided on the latter. She passed a cop and held up a dollar and said, "Vendor machine broke, I'll be back."

He shook his head nonchalantly as if he could care less because his focus was on a fellow brother in blue, that was all she needed to encourage herself to get the heck out of there. In the elevator she counted the money she had left on her, the forty she had on her gave her the answer she needed. She decided to head to her lover's house and lay low until she could figure out where she could go next. She knew that no one knew of the place. As she stepped outside she looked around to see if anyone was watching her but she knew that the hospital was too hot and the killer would not come back until everything had died down. She walked over to the cab, stood in front of the Bus Station around the corner from the hospital, and took a taxi to Mario's house.

As Michelle drew closer to Mario's a thought popped into her head, what if her Uncle was there? what if he blamed her what if he knew where Mario had relocated to?

She decided to knock on the door first and if he answered she would come in and explain her situation and say she just wanted to get her stuff she left there but she knew had to get to his room it would help set her next plan in motion.

CHAPTER FIVE
"Home?"

As Michelle pulled up to the house, she didn't see any foreign vehicles and prayed that everything was the way Mario had left it, especially never locking the side door. She still decided to knock and ring just in case.

She paid the taxi driver and got out of the car and silently said a prayer. She joked a little and inwardly said, "See Mario, I'm even starting to pray."

She walked up to the front door and knocked with no response she knocked gently at first then a little louder. She looked around although the houses were far apart she wanted to make sure she brought no attention to herself. When she was sure no one was there she went around to the side and tried the door and was relieved to see the door was open- this assured her that no one had come here.

Michelle walked into a flood of memories. So much so that she had to sit down to compose herself. The only thing Michelle wanted to do was sleep, she ran to the "closet." It was more of a little cut away behind the nightstand that Mario had put in place in case some one found out he wasn't the drug dealer they had thought he was and came to rob him. In this area was two bags - one filled with money and the other filled with Mario's , she couldn't bear to throw his out so she just added her clothes she left at his house.

Michelle pulled out her pajamas and underwear and went to the bathroom she filled up the tub and sank in the tub and grieved the love and memory of her true love and her Grandma E.

Michelle drifted into bed and sunk beneath the covers on Mario's side, his pillow still carried his scent and the bed was strangely warm and welcoming. She instantly fell asleep but her sleep was far from tumultuous she was being chased all through her city by this eye. Then there was Mario, soothing her and telling her it was going to be okay as he was there, she reached out to Mario it felt so real when Michelle finally awoke she was sitting in an upright position with her arms out. She yelled "Mario it's not ok. You're gone, Grandma E is gone, and I don't know why and by who". Michelle laid back down in despair as she realized she is in this world by herself.

Over the next week, Michelle realized that the comfort she thought she would get at Mario's was not going to happen. She decided not to go to Grandma E's funeral because whoever was trying to kill her would be there and follow her here and she would never be found. She pondered going back to school for some days now and decided that it would be safe because she now felt like she was in prison. She would get her degree and then move to another state and just wait for all this to die down.

The two and half hour ride helped ease some of her tension. Michelle had to remind herself to always stay cautious while there. She only had three months to go, then off to her new life.

Michelle took a necklace from Mario to wear around her neck in Remembrance of him which she vowed to never take off. She took a dare to go over to Grandma E's house but decided against it because she was sure her Mother, or worse, the killer was watching the house. She shed a tear at the thought that she only had memories of Grandma E and nothing tangible.

Michelle's heartbeat doubled as she pulled up into the school's parking lot. She didn't think past anything but staying here to complete school. She started to wish that she had fallen in love with Jesus as Mario had, then she would be able to talk to Him, like Mario and Grandma E always seemed to. She did say a short little prayer asking God to give her a little sign of what to do.

"Nothing" no reply. She got out of the car and suddenly thought about taking her bag and clothes out of Mario's car she "borrowed". She cautiously stepped out of the car and was quickly met with he chants of the students in the stadium area who were protesting another cop killing.

Michelle kept her head low as she made her way to her dorm. As she entered her roommate jumped up scaring Michelle. "Oh my God, Michelle, I heard about your grandma, how have you been? Was she sick or was it an accident,shrilled, Michelle's roommate Katie. Michelle made her way to her side of the room and lay on the bed.

"I'm okay?" Michelle squeaked out, She just wanted this to be a memory. She tried to drown out Katie's outpouring of love and continuous chatter.

"When your cousin told us we were so saddened and shocked, we just - Michelle cut off Katie mid-sentence "My cousin?"

"Yes Lanie, she came up here to check on you."

Michelle jumped up and started going into her closet and gathering clothes. "Umm, Lanie is my mother's name how did she look?" Michelle yelled at Katie.

Katie jumped and looked as if she was about to run out the door.

"I'm sorry" Michelle calmed down, "just been on edge." Lamented Michelle. "Are you sure everything's okay? Because your cousin just went to the store, she'll be back any moment."

"Look Katie, I can't explain it all, but she is very dangerous." Michelle started to collect some items while she thought what was her next move.

Michelle paced the floor as she tried to think, then said, "Katie remember that guy you used on campus who made your ID to get in the club, can you give me his number, please? I need him right now and please don't tell my cousin I've been here call the cops if she shows back up, please!"

Katie whipped out her phone and called Scotty and told him that Michelle would be on her way and she needed him asap "Life and death," is what she said Michelle thought to herself as she fled out the door if only she knew how true that statement was.

Michelle made her way to the steps if, in fact, her "cousin" was indeed on her way back from the store she figured she did not want to meet her on the elevator. Michelle immediately had to switch her mind off to figure out who was so set on harming her and to know she used her mother's name, was this an enemy of my mom's set out to exact revenge on me? Michelle pondered, she made her way out the side fire doors praying that the alarm wouldn't sound and bring attention to herself. No alarm rang, except in her mind. The only thing she was met with was beautiful sunlight and a small group of people had formed in the "yard" ,as it was known, to discuss the current events of the University.

The blaring of the music and the smell of activism in the air made Michelle wish things were so simple and that she could partake. But that wasn't the case and fear set in, it was almost as if she felt the moment the killer may have walked back on campus. She ran over to the athletic dorm where Katie informed Michelle that Scott lived.

Scott was in his dorm waiting for Michelle ready for "business." It was reminiscent of the usual spy movie and Michelle felt like she was in the movie where she encountered the computer nerd who had all the answers, except this was real life and Scott was far from the Geek Squad.

"Okay, so did you pick a new name or should I make one up?" Scott intervened in her little movie scenario going on in her mind.

"You can just make one up."

"Okay," he jumped excitedly at the thought of creating a new life for someone.

"What about Anquisha or something along those lines?" "Um," Michelle responded feeling a little offended and angry. She thought a little and out blurted "Rocky," thinking of the day that changed her life and decided this time it will be another change but for the better, "But with an I, and make my last name Richardson," she completed. It felt right to take on Mario's last name.

"And I want my age to reflect twenty-one like I'm fresh out of college." Michelle felt a little courage rising as the realization of a new name and a change was coming. Michelle's courage dissipated as she made her way back to the dorm to try and thank Katie and say goodbye as she made her way across the yard she saw the killer with this mask on her face and hoodie on that Michelle knew it was her in the glass-enclosed steps of her dorm and she was making her way down at such a pace that Michelle knew Katie was already gone. She clutched her new identity tighter to her and whispered, "Rocki."

She eyed her car which was but a short distance from the Killer who was sure to come out any moment. She needed a moment to think and she prayed, "Lord please cover me. Grandma E and Mario please have God send protection," she didn't know how effective this could have been because the protesters that were forming in the courtyard when she was heading to Scott's dorm were now making their way around the campus and the chant of "Black Lives Matter!" and "Defund the police," were getting stronger.

All Michelle could do was duck as the door swung open and at the exact time, she was engulfed in protestors which allowed her to make her way to the car unnoticed. She mouthed a silent but heartfelt thank you to God as she made her way to freedom and away from her past. She watched in the rear room as the killer made her way to the dorm but she knew she wouldn't get anything as Scott left out the room with her.

Michelle, no- Rocki thought, "I can finally be ahead of this instead of behind." She glanced once again in her rear view once again to the open road behind her and the promise of a new start sin front of her.

CHAPTER 6

Rocki! Rocki!

"Rocki! Rocki! Rocki!" The chant from the crowd made Rocki climb higher. Although this was exciting and arousing in most cases, Rocki felt like the higher she climbed up the pole, the further away she would get from her feelings of disgust for these people and the closer to heaven she got. She knew she would eventually have to come down, but she paused and made hand and foot movements which always drove the drunk heathen-infested crowd crazy. Even in her drunken state, she knew that she had to make her descent.

Much to the pleasure of the crowd, Rocki slowly made her way halfway down and then without notice dropped and ended in a split. The crowd went wild and Rocki was able to gather as much money as her arms would possibly allow and quickly make her exit stage. She ran to the "safety" of the basement and did what she always did before going back up to finish the night off with the lap dances for more money, she cried, the tears were not as hard as each day/night passed, but tonight her realizing that she was getting accustomed to this lifestyle brought on another round of tears.

By the time she finished with her pity party, she looked around the now empty room as she made her way upstairs. As she began her ascent to Hell her legs began to get heavy her breathing became erratic and she ran back down the steps and out the door, she ran the long trek to her car, her boss Vito complained so often about the workers taking up space for customers that she gave in and started parking around the corner. She finally made it to her car as the first spattering of rain began. She sat for a few moments and imagined the rain cleansing her of the "sins" of the past three years. Tears began again as Rocki began to reminisce.

Since placing the killer in her rearview, Rocki felt her storm finally passing. She laid low for six months at a hotel before she ended up in four cities over each state she stayed for a year and a half not laying roots just trying to see if she could, but she didn't feel comfortable until now. Although she had the money, she "borrowed", from Mario, and the last of what she had in her old bank account.

Miche- Rocki (who had to keep reminding herself of her new name) took a job as a waitress to establish herself enough to get an apartment, the money ran out in two years because the job didn't last much longer. She had met some of the strippers in the Diner she had worked in. One of those all-nighters after the Club joints… The Strippers would come there to giggle and complain, although Michelle always wondered why they didn't just go straight home she just minded her business, kept her head down, and kept racking up their ridiculous tips. They were so generous and although Rocki tried to stay out of their way they always requested for her and they used to comment to the point of harassment about Rocki coming to work with them.

"As pretty as you is," was one of their favorite lines, and then finally when she took them up on their offer it became, "she ain't all that." Rocki sank as far as she could in her seat and continued to let her mind wander ... So many men offering big cash in hopes she will look their way and be "extra nice" to them. But Rocki imagined Mario every night to make herself sensual enough, she imagined his caress, his lips, and his cologne. The thought of Mario made Rocki put her hands over her eyes and scream, "Lord deliver me from this." Something she often heard Grandma E cry out.

When she opened her eyes, dawn had broken and the sun had shone on her face, she imagined God saying, "I got you," and she turned her head to the left and imagined Grandma E was standing there ... the knock on the window jarred her she grabbed her head as she realized Grandma E?! was knocking on her window! Rocki pinched herself to see if she was asleep or worse... the tapping on her window commenced and there stood an older lady with the sweetest smile. Rocki rolled the window down halfway. "Baby I didn't mean to scare you I was coming out of my car and heard you screaming and wanted to make sure you were okay. Is everything okay?"

Yes, ma'am, I'm okay." Rocki stammered.

"Ok, she replied, I go to that church right over there. I'm there Monday -Sunday," she boasted with pride, "my name is Ms, Edna by the way." Looking down at Rocki's choice of apparel she glanced at the Eruption sign on the strip club Rocki worked and said, "I'll let you get to where you need to go." Rocki rolled the window down and grabbed her arm in desperation.

"My name is Michelle," she blurted out. For some reason she didn't want the lady to leave, she felt the peace that surrounded her and needed to hold on to it for as long as she could. The lady smiled again she reached into her purse and gave Michelle a card "Baby it's ok, if you need anything, something to eat, a job, or just to talk I'm here Monday through Sunday. Ok, I will be seeing you, ok?" Michelle looked down at the card and looked up again to say thank you and she was gone.

"Thank you, Grandma E, and thank you, God," she mouthed thinking she just had an encounter with an angel.

Rocki's encounter as she called was what she needed to quit Club Eruption and use her fake degree to apply for an entry-level job at the news network. She was hired immediately to work as a Production Desk Assistant, which had such a weighty title but Rocki soon found out it was the equivalent of a paid Intern and although the pay didn't even come close to what she made at Eruption; to be able to feel that Grandma E and Mario were proudly watching her slowly becoming, brought a feeling that a million dollars couldn't compare to. Rocki decided to take the money she had saved up and paid up her Condo for a year and her bills for up to six months to keep her ahead this time. She felt the shift in her life and was ready for whatever came her way.

"O what a beautiful morning; O what a beautiful day!" Rocki felt like singing this song from the top of a mountain. Although she just got out of bed she knew the day would be a beautiful one. She was getting further away from Michelle and her past, now she felt like Rocki was taking over and conquering everything and she felt just plain safer. Although she hadn't taken

Ms. E- that's what she called her now, up on her offer to come visit her church, Rocki felt her life was better since she came across her Angel. She started to see Ms. E often at the market, the mall, and even at the news station when she came to protest about the cops not doing anything to close down those establishments around the Church that had people scared to come to Church. She was quite the activist. Rocki wanted so badly to just get to know Ms. E more but she was scared that getting close to her was like giving her the death Penalty. But today she felt differently, if she ran into her she may invite her to lunch. She felt different even the cute cameraman that kept "nagging " her for a date may get a," we'll see.

CHAPTER 7
Where there is smoke …

Today Rocki woke with a foreboding sense of doom. Mario came to her in her dreams warning her to be cautious. Rocki woke up ready to call in and not go to work especially since she felt such an urgency in making the call as if some unforeseen force was pushing her. But it was like Grandma E's voice came in loud and clear and pushed Rocki out of bed into the living room where she kept Grandma E's Bible- the only memory, reminder, and proof of her existence.

Michelle picked up the Bible and just looked at the cover she started to think about any scripture to read to help her sort through her thoughts. She leaned back on the sofa and immediately allowed herself to think about Grandma E. Although her name conjured up the Grandma sitting on the front porch with her housecoat on. Grandma E was quite the opposite. Beautifully caramel-complected, strong jawline from years of setting her face like stone and just getting the job done. She looked young for her age as she was told often and although she had the stern voice like a librarian, she had the softest touch when Michelle needed it, the greatest hugs at the right time. And the greatest listener with the best advice. And because Rocki was in awe of how Grandma E just lived her day "on God's grace" she often stated. Rocki took and tried to hold on to every bit of advice that Grandma E gave her. She wanted so bad to walk in her shoes. Rocki sat down the Bible a little roughly, Why did her life have to end like that and because of her? She assumed. She let the tears wash over her face as she thought of what Grandma E endured. Rocki left so hastily she didnt get all the facts but she knew Grandma E ain't going down without a fight. Rocki had a sudden thought, what if she died to protect her?

She picked the Bible up and remembered Grandma E saying "Michelle, people get it so confused Heaven is our goal, and no matter how we make it there, that is the goal. Death is not the end but the most beautiful beginning." It gave Michelle comfort knowing

Grandma E was finally there, she knew without a doubt, she made it in.

Rocki had a sudden thought, she ran and got her phone and looked up the word and googled where is the word Greater in the Bible. A long list of Scriptures came up but the first one she came to was I John 4:4, she ran and got her Bible. She wanted to read it from the Bible not the phone. She read, "Ye are of God, little children, and have overcome them: because Greater is He that is in you then he that is in this world."

For some reason this made the tears come even more. She held the Bible to her chest and prayed that God would be great in her today and protect her from anything that the devil had set in her path. Rocki felt she had to believe that no weapon would prosper and that she would be ok no matter what today brought.

She showered and got ready for the day. The shower washed away her before feeling of doom and gloom as she played one of her favorite Clark Sisters songs, "Trust in Him" and ended with "You Brought the Sunshine." There was no way you could stay in a funk after listening to those songs. She made it to work early and took that time to clean out her desk from all the candy she ate to stay awake during long nights and note pads of brief reminders, varying from pick up clothes from the cleaners mtg at 4 to affirmations of "you are going to make it" she sifted through the mass of posts to see which to keep or redo because some had turned into coasters and bearded the stains of the coffee from a mug. The way Rocki's desk was situated she had to put a mirror up just in case she was needed and had her back to the newsroom. Because of this, she saw Michael approaching she pretended as if she was still cleaning but she was aware of his presence approaching. Michael was in every word the cameraman, but he actually worked in HR. For some reason, he longed to be in the everyday chaos of the newsroom and chose the task of working the cameras. Michael was 6'5 or something like that just right for her 5'4" height. He was the model type, mixed with just the right amount of street to make him not appear stand-offish and approachable.

He smelled of outdoors mixed with musk and soft echoes of sandalwood. And the dimples had her fixated every time he talked. The only flaw was the faint limp that gave him a mysterious aura, but, added to his masculinity. In the time he was walking over Rocki had to talk herself into engaging with him because she felt as if she was somehow being disloyal to Mario, when someone's life is cut short and just abruptly ended you still wait for them to walk through the door, a phone call asking if you want something from the store. Although her heart ached, longed and agonized over the thought of Mario really being gone, logic constantly reminded her of his non existence. It was this logic that told her to move on and be open to a new normal life. Michael tried many times to strike up a conversation and she brushed him aside which she could tell shocked him. She was sure that he was very sure of himself. She laughed at how he had blurted out, "Can I take you out?" before she could avoid conversation with him. She politely declined and felt bad because he kept looking back at her like a wounded puppy that just wanted a belly rub. She silently apologized to him that day and then later apologized to herself because she was now bored the whole weekend.

Michael finally made his way up to the desk and when Rocki turned she saw he had a cupcake with a candle on top. He and a few other coworkers began singing as off key as you could guess "Happy Birthday to you." Michelle was about to join in when she realized it was meant for her. She was a little taken aback because she had put the first date that came to mind.

"How did you know?" She mouthed to Michael.

"I'm in HR, it's my job to know. It looked like you forgot for a moment," he chuckled.

"How old are you?" Exclaimed a Co-Worker.

One of the Front Desk Anchors stated, "Now you know a woman never tells that."

The banter between the coworker and Front desk Anchor gave Rocki time to compose herself fully under Michael's watchful glaze.

"Thank you, everyone " that was so kind of you. She took an obligatory bite of the cupcake and everyone applauded as if she was five. Michael chimed in, "hey its the weekend lets celebrate after work."

Dan the other cameraman jokingly said, "us too Mike."

"Of course, everyone" Michael jokingly reprimanded. Rocki shook her head and said, "No please don't make a fuss,"

Michael shook his head and said, "No we aren't taking no for an answer. You have to get out sometime."

"Its time" Michael mouthed but Mario's voice came out. Rocki hung her head and looked up and stated "ok I'll go." "Mazel tov," someone raved and everyone laughed as the work day began.

The News Room was alive and jumping today. Breaking News after Breaking News was coming in. Rocki was beginning to regret her accepting the invitation. But every time she would look up to tell Michael she had changed her mind he had such a grin on his face and gave her the thumbs up. She dared not rain on his parade.

5:00 came so fast and Michael was ready to leave and go home. She dashed to the restroom to refresh her makeup and have a one-on-one, "Pep Talk."

Part of her hoped that by the time she came back to the newsroom would be empty and they forgot her, and the other part was scared that when she came back to the newsroom would be empty and they forgot about her and was gone to party. She walked out of the restroom with her eyes closed. Micheal's laugh as she was exiting brought on a sigh of relief or a sigh of exasperation. Rocki thought she will figure out which one it was later.

POCO's was a beautiful hole in the wall with a back-home vibe. It was too updated to be an exact hole in the wall but not enough to be 4-star. An easy 3.5 stars at the most. But it was like a "where everyone knows your name" place. The music was blasting enough to make you get up and dance but not enough were you can't have a decent conversation.

Rocki decided this was the perfect place to let her hair down. She was so caught up in the vibe of the moment that she hadn't realized she was swaying to the music and had actually taken down the mock bun she created earlier as she was hustling through the Newsroom. It was only when she went to take a sip of her drink that she saw or maybe felt Michael's eyes on her. Not just a "oh she's enjoying herself" look. But as if he was mesmerized and was memorizing everything about her.

A chill ran through her and she almost choked on her drink as he licked his lips. Lord this was a Sprite, why was she reeling? She tried to conjure up Mario's face to squelch the feeling that was coming over her. But she kept seeing Michael's dimples and imagined what was under that shirt in those jeans... She tried so hard to see Mario's face and felt hopeless as if she was in a scene from Titanic and her love was floating away to become a distant memory. Micheal's gentle booming voice invaded her thoughts, "It's ok I can bring you back whenever." he whispered across the back of her neck as he came up behind her.

"Huh," she breathlessly exclaimed.

"You looked as if you were trying hard to remember each moment and your face was so squinched up," he stated as he mocked her face. Rocki playfully swatted at his chest at the made-up word and his mocking, but she let her hand linger from his chest and then rested on his arm. She closed her eyes so he would not see the fire that she was sure was in her eyes. When she did, she saw the same fire in his. She backed up and smooth her hands over her clothes.

Michael still had that smoldering look in his eyes "It's ok I don't mind waiting, Rocki, you're worth the wait."

Michael grabbed her up to dance to the slow tune that was playing and just as they reached the floor an upbeat classic came over the speakers. She laughed inwardly at the thought Mario was being jealous.

The walk home was for lack of any words, delicious. Michael was so animated as he talked. She was so caught up in his voice she didn't hear his words. "Where are you from? I can tell your accent is not Midwest are you from down south or east coast?"

Rocki froze like a deer in headlights; she forgot about this, the getting-to-know-you phase of a relationship. She didn't practice anything because her goal was to keep her head low, not date, and stay alive.

"You guessed right." she stammered.

Michael looked at her confused "how?" he responded.

Quickly thinking and thanking the geography gods, she said, "I'm from a small town right on the Mason-Dixon line and east coast so we are considered both."

Before he could ask anything else she started to pummel Michael with questions. By the time they landed at her doorstep, he was worn out.

"Looks like we are here."

"How do you know?' she asked trying to downplay the fear and lump in her throat.

"You are standing on the step, you stopped, and you're looking for your keys I presume?" Gesturing to her subconsciously going through her purse.

He then continued, "Calm down I haven't been stalking you, except to get your birthday," putting his hands up in surrender.

"Aww, man I wanted to try out that new can of mace I purchased" Rocki jokingly countered.

Michael backed up and said, "I'm scared of you," his voice changed as he walked forward and asked, "Should I be?" "Of course not "Rocki looked up at him not realizing the pleading in her eyes that made him now feel an unrecognizable lump in his throat.

"Should I be afraid of you Michael? You seem too good to be true." He reached down and planted a kiss on her cheek. "Are you trying to distract me, are you too good to be true?" and with that he walked away.

Rocki felt a new loneliness when she walked through her door. She wanted to invite Michael in but this was the sanctuary where she could think of Mario and Grandma E. But when she walked in the door she felt as if Mario was gone and now she didn't have his memories nor Michael here. She tried to ignore the chill that ran through her as she thought of Michael. He had a little bit of a dangerous aura to him. She laughed at that as if she was a Psychic. She quickly sobered at the thought it could be the discernment Grandma E talked about and the Bible telling us that God always gives warnings and if we don't heed the warning and fall into this temptation, God will make a way for us to escape and bear the situation. Rocki held on to this. Could being too good to be true go both ways? But something in her didn't want to acknowledge which way her instinct was telling her...

Michael picked up the phone, from its incessant ringing, and looked at the clock. "Who is calling me at 2:45 am?!" He instantly became alert as he realized it was The Client. He answered the phone to his angry "client" screaming, "why haven't you called me? Your date ended hours ago, is it her?" The client angrily barraged him with questions.

"I'm not sure," Michael himself barked, he had to let this Client know he was in it for the money he wasn't scared even though talking with The Client always left his stomach in endless knots.

"I gave you everything you needed to know." the Client yelled "Ugh, are you still running the clip next week?"

"Yes," he said in exasperation, "and if she gives any hint that it's her I will call the polic…"

"NOOOO" the client interrupted, "you will do no such thing. You will call me and I will handle it. I have not patiently waited all these years for you to mess things up." The Client growled. "Look, Micheal growled back. I'm not sure if she is who you are looking for but it is my duty to call the police. She doesn't even seem like the type to even be caught up in whatever you are in. I think the best thing—-," Micheal appealed.

"…is for you to do what I paid you to do nothing more." The Client calmly interrupted then disconnected the line.

CHAPTER 8

◆Interlude ...

Rocki felt as if Michael was doing his best to prove he was too good without making her feel that it couldn't be true. Rocki's Friday night outing left her bold enough to call Michael and invite him to a post-birthday outing. This invitation took him somewhere she hadn't been in years, skating. "Nothing will show how a person is more than when they are in survival mode." Michelle jokingly thought.

Then she became somber at the thought that has been her mode since she was 18. She shook her head to stop her train of thought. When she came into the house she decided to read Grandma E's bible, because she didn't know where to start she decided to just look at Grandma E's bookmark and the first scripture said "No weapon formed against her would prosper."

She prayed "Lord I don't want them to even form!"

The next one she came to was the Lord's Prayer she knew that.

The next page she turned to oddly also had a pic of her and Mario, the cheesy ones you take at the State Fair to show your "real love" for one another. The Scripture that it bookmarked was really a plea, "Philippians 3:12 Forgetting those things which are behind and press towards the call of God."

Rocki realized she had to let the past go because nothing could change it. she took a shirt that she had of Mario and a handkerchief of Grandma E and placed the ashes in an urn necklace she had brought online to put a memento of them but she had to go on the run before either of their funeral. Rocki knew a part of her had died with them. But Michael gave her hope that she still had a reason to live and have peace in the situation. She went back and recited the Lord's Prayer not only with her lips but with her heart and then thanked God and took solace that although the weapon formed. it wouldn't prosper. She went to bed with that very comfort and woke up emboldened.

Rocki picked up the phone to call the very person who led her to even read the Bible: Michael.

He answered so quickly as if he was waiting for the call. "Hello," Michael answered in an almost singsong voice. Silence Michael went on alert for some reason his heart was beating erratically at the thought the Client may have gotten to Rocki before he could really get to know what exactly was going on.

"Hello?" Rocki now lost her boldness at his voice, there goes that crazy feeling in her gut. She realized it was butterflies and the fear of rejection from Michael if he didn't want to go on another "outing".

"Hello." Rocki stammered, "Just seeing how you are doing today." I'm good, Micheal exclaimed, but the only way to know if I am telling the truth is to see for yourself, would you like to go out again?" Michelle boldly stated, "Yes, I know the perfect place if you are up to a blind excursion."

Michael proved in every way he was up to the challenge. Rocki didn't remember his limp until he picked her up and got out of the car to open the car door {which melted her heart by the way} then she felt guilty and thought the invite might become offensive. She bit her nail anxiously and Michael, being the observant person he was, asked, "Why you so nervous, Rocki?" "I'm so sorry Michelle blurted out, we are going skating, I forgot about your leg…your limp." She felt like a run-on sentence. Michael grabbed her hand in his. Rocki looked up into his eyes and something clicked and it seemed like it happened for both of them, they both looked away shocked.

Michael came up first, "Rocki, it's okay I really believe you mean no ill for me. My leg does not bother me in the least. Let's make sure you can keep up," he laughed. "Oh yeah? she jokingly retorted she tried to say more but she as a woman could not jump so easily to the mutual spark they just shared and now she was tasked (self-imposed) to figure out what it meant.

The ride to the "Spinning Wheels" skating rink was by some standards chatty. Michael without asking questions was able to pull info from Rocki. Rocki was careful not to let Michelle's information come out, even though she felt guilty about this; she realized it was to protect him more than herself. And for some reason, she felt like everything she said put Michael at ease. Remembering how Grandma E used to tell her to use the discernment God had given her after that near-death beating she received in High School. "It will get you out of a lot of trouble, it's putting it in God's hands, and it almost is like Him giving you this reward by showing you the way out for trusting and believing in him." She had explained in laymen's terms.

Almost like a "Christ for dummies Crash Course" is how Michelle always felt after those "talks."

Michael brought her back from her trip down memory lane. "We are finally here, feels like a school trip, let's pray." Rocki looked up as she grabbed his hand. Michael who was joking saw the sincerity in her gesture so he said a quick prayer. He stumbled because this was something he hadn't done in a long time not since ... he shook the memory from his mind. No more conversations were had between them as

Michael and Rocki got to the task at hand, skating. Michael proved to be just as smooth on the rink as he was in the newsroom, maybe smoother. He was so sure of himself that she noticed his limp all but disappeared. Now she couldn't say the same for herself. If it wasn't for Michael's strong hands guiding her around the ring she would've fell for sure.

He became her teacher, and she imagined all the other things she could learn from him. She took advantage when the DJ called for all couples to skate and an old-school classic came from the speakers. She let her hands linger on his chest and arms. She looked into his eyes and opened herself up so he could see her soul, her joy at meeting him, needing him, and wanting him... he answered by lowering his head to kiss her, and then the blare from the fire alarm went off and broke the trance.

Michael laughed but then looked around, as if ,he was on high alert or at least that was the only thing that came to Rocki's mind. She had seen this look on Mario many times they had gone out, it was as if he was always making sure she was safe. Rocki touched his hand. "It's okay" she reassured Michael, "let's go get something to eat," she said as she led him off the Rink.

Michael knew from his short time on the force that this was no coincidence. He looked around for any traces of the Client. Because he never saw her up close he had no idea how she looked plus she always wore that ugly hoodie. And today would have been out of place on this lovely day. He thought he glanced at someone exiting to the far left of the Rink with a hoody, but the once half-empty Rink was at capacity and made it more difficult to see. Michael looked down as Rocki grabbed his hand and told him It was ok. And he knew with everything in him he would make sure she was always ok.

The Client felt like throwing up watching Micheal and Michelle skate. Knowing something didn't sound right in his voice. Michael was gyrating on the skating rink. The Client felt as if it was episode One of a dating reality show. Michael was not being paid to find love, he had to keep his head in the game.

The client reached into the hoodie to feel the cold steel of the gun but felt that would bring too much attention.

Although this became more of a delicious game, the Client was tired of killing unnecessarily, While Michelle got away.

This time, patience, was needed to exact the perfect revenge needed. The Client became so caught up in the past. The sleepless nights the torment exacted because of the loss of love. Sometimes when there were no leads the Client decided maybe just let it go and just live a normal life, and quickly erased that thought. Nothing was normal since that day! Michelle ruined so many lives on that one day! The surge of anger bought the Client out of a daze and decided to go out and skate close enough to see. It sort of looked like Michelle, sThe Client could almost smell the desperation and dejection caused by Michelle's life on the run which brought great joy from the Client. But she did not look like Michelle in the physical sense.

They had both grown in looks and the Client had no leads for six years until the use of Michelle's ATM card a year ago alerted police at the station the client worked as a front desk clerk to keep one step ahead. Although the police felt Michelle didn't put down roots. The Client felt a pull to this place. So as not to alert anyone, the client hired Micheal an old former police officer who barely made it out of the Academy before tragedy struck and he left the force. And was now working as a Private Investigator. And here he is, making out with the supposed suspect as the Client made her out to be. The Client looked around for another diversion and saw the fire alarm.

"Real lame TV storyline," the Client thought as the lever was pulled down. The Client paced quickened someone upstairs must really be looking out for that girl. Too many misses and the Client didn't like to lose. The Client was ready for this to be over so life could begin. The side entrance was The Clients quickest means of escape without being noticed and had to get back to the hotel to remove the nasty ink left from ringing the alarm.

Michelle choose Poco again the same restaurant where the 'birthday" celebration was held. She loved the feel and anonymity it brought while feeling as if she belonged there at that moment whenever she walked through the door. She decided to eat something different off the menu each time they [or if she just came by herself], entered the restaurant until she was able to tell the waitress, bring me my usual". She relished in that thought and looking over at Michael, prayed he was there whenever she reached that benchmark. Could this be a new beginning? Please, she prayed, she was tired of running. She wanted somewhere to feel at home, someone to feel at home with. Micheal was bringing on a revival of feelings. Feelings, she honestly felt were no longer available to her especially, with the death of Mario and Grandma E. She felt she had reached her limit.

" I told you to get the steak." Micheal brought her out her musings. "It will surprise you, Next time we come," Michelle quipped. "Ohhhh, next time, I like the sound of that. Tell me a little about yourself

Rocki." Rocki became so nervous. What do you want to know?" She bumbled out. "What is your favorite color and food?" Michael asked, trying to steer clear of the past. He had decided on the ride to Poco's that he didn't wanna know. He was now Michelle or Rocki if that is the name she chooses, her protector not hunter. His only quandary was whether should he tell Rocki what he knew, scared that it might push her away, or not tell her and be scared she would find out and, then pushes him away.

Michelle sat and watched the range of motions across Michael's face. Whatever he was caught up in, was the same look of fear when the alarm went off. Rocki realized maybe Michael was battling his own past. Even though now she was curious. But if she asked him, she would have to tell her story . That was something she wasn't ready to do. She only had an instinct discernment to believe he really is on the good side. The way he protected her at the Rink, left her believing she was in good company.

"Where did you go?" Micheal interrupted, "You went into another world; locked in your thoughts. Is everything okay?"

He looked so sincere and honest, Rocki thought. Rocki exhaled about to spill her guts when divine intervention in the form of a phone rang. Michael inwardly cursed, and at the same time breathed a sigh of relief. But the person on the other end made him inwardly curse again. He decided to ignore the call and sent a text; *No info yet will let you know after the story is running.* He sent the text and waited for a response. The Client texted back simply. *"Ok."*

He breathed, which gave him a day and a half to come up with a plan to get them to safety. He put his phone away as he exhaled and took a sharp intake of fresh air, that new air represented a new beginning.

"You know what, Rocki?" he said interrupting his thoughts "no more questions, I want everything you tell me to be because you trust that I got you, and it comes organically, whatever that means."They both breathed a sigh of relief. "Here is to letting it come organically," Michelle chimed in clinking his glass.

Sunday came without incident, Michael thought he had to make today the *bestest* day ever, even if that wasn't a word. Today he has to make her believe in him. He decided no matter what happened on Monday, when the show aired he was team Rocki and he needed her to know it. He still had this gnawing in his stomach because the advantage "The Client" had over him was that he had never seen The Client's face. Even when he was in the Client's presence the voice was always robotic as if they wore some sort of device to alter their voice. Majority of their interactions were through email. He paused at this thought; maybe he can get one of his buddies form the force to keep track of the client's IP address. This way he could at least stay in the know of the Clients whereabouts. He put that on his mental weekly to-do list. But looking across at Rocki, he placed it high on his priorities of things to do. He had decided he wanted to spend the whole day and ... possibly the night with Rocki. He had to convince himself it was more for safety reasons then the throbbing that took place every time since he first met her. But the anticipation of knowing that was going to eventually happen, gave him that gentleman's patience.

It felt like a supernatural power when you realized you had to acquire that virtue, he chuckled inwardly as he pictured himself putting on his superhero cape with a big "P" on it for patience . He burst out laughing in his mind, and in real life. "Now it's your turn to tell me where you went" Michelle softly chuckled along.

"Nope." Micheal said shaking his head emphatically, "Remember, organically, when the time comes."

Michelle looked around the empty picnic area that Michael had chosen for their Sunday rendezvous. The spread of food let her see he was thinking about things that she liked from what she brought to the work place. Rocki tossed and turned all night. While the Skating Rink had been a flop; the rest of the evening solidified her feeling that it was time to move on, still keeping the beautiful memory of Mario and the standard he set in loving her, but knowing she won't ever receive that love from him any longer. Michael was proving that he was man enough to fill that spot. He had called her early on Sunday morning and told her just prepare for a long day. "Operation win your heart." is what he called it. She laughed at him making his intentions known. One thing she said she wanted in any man crossing her path was the ability to communicate because Mario had shown her the importance of it. So much so she was able to decipher what he required from her on the days when he wasn't communicative. After the picnic, Michael said he just wanted to walk without thinking of anything but the moment they were in .

"What are you running from?" Rocki couldn't help but think as they walked waked along the waterfront. People were starting to mill around and they came upon the 2-hour cruise that was docked at the end of the Pier.

Michelle squeaked "I always wanted to go on those boats.; Maybe that will be our next adventure."

"There is no time like the present," Michael said with a straight face. Presenting two tickets out of his perfectly pressed shirt. He had to run there early that morning to get the tickets although it was someone's reunion he took the tickets he didn't care about the details. It would be just him and Rocki as far as he was concerned. And concerned he was because it turned out to be a 6oth class reunion and he had never seen so many electric wheelchairs ,and walkers in his life.

Michelle could not contain her excitement and laughter as she took in the scene around her. And Michael's dejected face.

"I'm sorry Rocki, maybe we can exchange the tickets for next Sunday," he soberly stated.

Michelle objected "No, I want to go we may have more fun than we ever had." Remembering all the fun she had with the new Grandma E.

As they were boarding Rocki's perfume and Michael's cologne were now being replaced with the smell of ointment, and peppermint. Rocki looked over and felt someone watching her. She shook her head at the thought but grabbed Michael's hand for assurance that he was right by her side.

The atmosphere was energetic on the cruise. The drinks were flowing everyone was vibing. And it was safe to say, Michael, on the dance floor taking turns dancing with every white-haired lady on the floor, was having a good time. Rocki, who had sat this round out was watching everything around her and she didn't know if it was the boat making her sway or the many rounds of drinks she had. She felt the most at peace right here. Now, she felt, at this moment, she could move on. She glanced over at Michael who was watching her so intently and beckoned her out on the floor. She shook her head saying "No," then she smiled and lifted her glass to show him she was getting another drink. He resumed his dancing. Rocki went to refresh her drink, as she was waiting for the refill from the bartender. Someone came behind her and she felt their presence but was too scared to turn for some reason. Then she heard her name being called and turned to her right and was looking straight in the eyes of Mrs E the lady from the church by her old job. she turned to the left to see who was the presence she felt but all she saw were the long lines of faces and silvery hair of people waiting for their drinks. Rocki turned all of her attention to her angel in human form. Because of Mrs. E's presence this time Rocki ordered her drink in virgin form. And Mrs. E beckoned Rocki to follow her to the table she was sitting at. Rocki was okay with this invitation, she still had a clear view of Michael on the dance floor. A slight twinge of guilt flooded Rocki momentarily but she came to her senses quickly as she realized he was just having fun and if he didn't waste his energy there it would've been on her to keep him entertained; and, by the way, he had been dancing which was something she would completely be unable to do.

"When are you coming to church?" Mrs. E asked interrupting Rocki's thoughts. Rocki took a moment to respond with everything going in her favor, Rocki kind of felt like it was only right to go and thank God for watching over her and keeping her safe. This could be like the next phase a new beginning.

"I will definitely be there soon,I promise" answered Rocki. "No need to promise me," remarked Mrs. E. "This is more for you than anyone else." Mrs. E looked towards the dance floor, and added, "Bring your friend too, okay?" As the song was ending and Michael was making his way towards them. Rocki and Mrs. E were immersed in chatter and laughing like old friends, "Who could that be?" thought Michael he slowed his steps to watch how Rocki and the lady seemed at ease with each other. "Could it be an old teacher or babysitter? Please let it be anybody that places Rocki as far away from being Michelle as possible," he inwardly pleaded. He had to find out more, he wanted to know … he *needed* to know.

Michael made his way over and lightly placed his hand on Rocki's back. Rocki turned and introduced Mrs. E to Michael."I was just inviting Rocki and you too of course to church".

Michael wanted to run as far as he could from the conversation, as far as he ran from church a long time ago, never to look back. But, to Rocki who was smiling from ear to ear, Michael tweaked out a small, "Of course, when?". Knowing he would be busy whenever.

As Mrs. E went on and on and on about the pros of coming to church, Both Michael and Rocki were both caught up in their own thoughts.

Had they both not been so engrossed in their own thoughts they would have been more cautious and seen that the boat had more than silver hair and oxygen tanks ...

Michael could only say the mood had soured, for him, at least. Here was this, Mrs. E, messing his peace and his plans to get a piece, all were being shot to Hell. She even had the nerve to pray for them, thank God, one of his silver angels pulled him away in the nick of time.

Although,he was still dancing with the silver fox, who had a problem keeping her hand to herself, he was a million miles away. He glanced over to Rocki and her angel who both had their heads bowed.

"Lord, how long is she gonna pray?" This was one of those Thanksgiving prayers his dad prayed every Sunday after he left the pulpit and they sat down for dinner. Flash backing to when Michael was a little boy; Michael thought his dad was Superman, and Santa all wrapped up in one. Michael would sit in the back church watching how everyone was mesmerized by his dad as he preached the Word of God. It wasn't until he was older that he realized how flawed his dad was. He saw his father preach the word and with that same booming voice continuously put his mom down until she couldn't take it anymore and ended her life. Michael still blamed his dad and himself. The guilt that, even though he blamed his dad in every way for his mom's death; he had to be the one who helped his dad back to recovery. And to add insult to injury and his shame, his dad gave all the credit to God.

Michael was the one who helped him shower, fed him, and was there to hold him when he cried himself to sleep consumed with the guilt of his wife taking her life and how people may have looked at him. His dad's love for God grew as Michael diminished. Although he had his moments he wanted to call on God, he suppressed it and tucked it away with the Easter Bunny and Santa Claus. So he knew, for Michelle's or Rocki's sake, it must have been divine intervention that placed him on her path. Last night was so beautiful he felt his destiny was stamped across it. The only thing he wished hadn't happened was the appearance and interference of Mrs. E. She was a beautiful woman, but he knew her kind sucked you into the "religion thing" and you couldn't shake off its hold on you. Had you missing out on living a fun life all to please a God who, in Michael's eyes, never returned the favor? But yet at the same time made you feel pleasingly captured and.... confused. There was not one day he thought how his mom can speak of God, and this God never gave her a flash of her child needing her and not think of what her dying left behind! At that moment, though Michael felt he was angrier at his mom than ... He quickly shook his head to erase that narrative. No, he knew that he had to blame God, he could've sent an angel a signal to his dad, him, or someone, right? He saw too much death depravity, and pain as a cop to realize that God gave up on "His" children a long time ago. But as Michael wiped the dew he wished he could go back to the day before it happened and fussed his dad out, wiped away her tear, and tell her he needed her. He looked in the mirror hovering over the bar and for a split second he saw the reflection of himself as a child, kneeling beside his mom just crying over her lifeless body, weeping, and all the pills scattered and his dad just standing there doing nothing, not praying, not screaming to God, nothing. He saw the lost little boy still crying in pain and also guilt for not being enough and also for helping keep the secret of how she died so his dad could keep his image. He angrily wiped again " It wasn't your job to take care of her either", he yelled to the little boy in him. He looked heavenward. "How can you allow me to go through so much pain? he raged inside. Every time he asked this question he pictured big hands tied behind their back in frustration. "Was God telling him his parents tied

God's hand or was he?" He was again left lost and confused so tormented by the train of thought sometimes he felt like he wanted to take the same route as his mom did. This alternative would have been an option months ago, but now, not so much. He would never put Rocki through that. Especially the unanswered questions suicide brings. So now here he was a grown man stuck with Daddy and Mommy issues, trapped in anger at a "loving" God, who he needed so much and yet felt so disconnected from, that it was better to not believe than to believe and be

disappointed. He cringed every time he came around those Holy Rollers like Mrs. E; So sweet on the outside, but inwardly and at home silently judging everyone but themselves.

He was so torn he did everything to avoid them like a Plague but then there were times he would pray they would see his hurt his pain and help him crack this code and go to the next level in God, becoming a new creature like he used to be. The part of him that wanted to avoid them showed up and he laughed. He just wanted it to be him and Rocki in a world by themselves, heavy PDA in effect. No one else mattered at the Skating Rink until the alarm. The buzz of the alarm made him feel like he was running out of time. Its glare interrupted his fairytale and brought him back to the reality that today determined a much-needed opened door to his destiny. Because he was a PI with a heart at least and for some reason he felt as if, for now, the least the Client knew, the better for Rocki. Good or Bad, he had Rocki's back.

Monday came and Michael went about watching Rocki as if she was fresh spun cotton candy. Although the piece was not to be played until after Lunch, he needed to see how she was during the day to compare against when she watched the news. She seemed fine but his nerves were shot and frazzled which left him short. He squawked at everyone who crossed his path. Which was highly unlike him. Even when Rocki came and checked on him after everybody made him the water cooler talk, it did nothing to ease his nerves.

Michael thought if he just stuck to the HR duties of his job instead of going to his office, he decided to create a makeshift desk on the newsroom floor. He had to be there to see her reaction and cover her if needed. He became so immersed in his work that the familiar jingle of Breaking news was almost missed but then his heart began to race as the anchorman on the monitor began…

"Although it may seem like a distant memory to some, the family of Elaine Chambers still want answers for the death of their beloved Grandmother, mother, and friend and for the safe return of her

granddaughter Michelle Harris. We are here Live with her daughter Lanie Chambers, Ms. Chambers, please let us know how you have been." The Camera cuts to Michelle's mom, who looks, for lack of a better word, tired. "I just want my daughter back, we're all we have left. She must be out there, I will not believe she is gone and if anyone knows anything please reach out to me, Michelle I'll never stop looking for you."

The anchorman returned and said, "Here is a picture of Michelle, who is not a suspect but wanted to answer questions not only for the death of her grandmother; but the shooting of Officer Gomez." As the camera cuts to a shot of Michelle, as a child, a coffee cup dropping to the floor, momentarily caught everyone's attention as Michelle just spilled the coffee all over herself. She had such a look of fear in her eyes as she looked helplessly at Michael.

This interaction was all The Client needed as she rushed to help clean up the mess that Michelle just made. It was after all The Clients first day on the job as a Grip slash Janitor. For The Client, today was a good day "Time." The Client inwardly whispered to herself, "Just give it time."

CHAPTER 9
"...There's fire"

Michelle could not explain the overwhelming grief that overtook her as she watched her grandmother's face on the monitor. She forced herself to memorize every detail as if that was the last time and she didn't see her face almost every night in her sleep. Her mother looked at every part of the worn-down loving mother who just wanted, no, *needed* her missing child back. But Michelle knew better. Her mother was far from loving, wanting, or needing! When the anchorman said she was wanted for questioning her body stopped functioning. To even suggest that she was a part of or had any knowledge of who took her grandmother's and Mario's lives and they didn't even say anything about Mario this time or ever. Was he just brushed off like another senseless killing in a senseless city? A part of her was angry at the thought of both, she had half a mind to turn herself in, just to give them a piece of her mind, but then the other half; the one linked to her fear and her skeletal system just as the anchorman stated a picture of her would be plastered on the monitor. Her heart lurched until she saw it was a picture of her at 5, her chubby self. They then did an age progression which bore a remarkable canniness to her. She turned so fast to escape the imagined recognition from her co-workers. Which in turn brought more attention, she tried to feign just simple clumsiness but when her eyes met Michael she felt like he knew.

She only had a moment to ponder as the janitor begrudgingly came and cleaned up muttering the whole time as he attended to the task of cleaning. She watched as Michael's face went from sympathy to disappointed. Why choose those responses, another wave of fear came over her, how did he know? Who did he know? Her thoughts were interrupted by the janitor, Michelle heard the janitor whisper just one word- "time," and Michelle agreed time would tell her everything.

Michelle shook herself from her fog and noticed that the newsroom went back to the same hustle and bustle, which calmed her because it appeared no one was even paying attention to the monitor.

"Wow, great," investigative and reporting, Michelle brooded. She sat down and for once thought about something she hadn't thought about in a long time … running again. She looked around again, calmed, and reassured herself that she was okay, except for Micheal, she looked over at him at his makeshift desk, his body language wasn't reading the on-edge angry bear he displayed earlier or the picture of doom and gloom during the breaking news. Maybe she just imagined, it maybe he's just going through stuff, he looked as if nothing just took place, as if her world wasn't just tossed upside down from a 3-minute news segment.

Michael was just sitting in the corner reading a paper, legs crossed, and drinking his coffee. He caught her watching him and winked. She smiled for the first time in the last 20 minutes and winked back. She turned away because that wink brought on new questions; should she tell him everything so that way he can help her?

"Selfish!" Came to her mind as she thought of how everyone that was even close to her was harmed. And also what would she say? "Hey, I just wanted you to know that I lied this whole time my name is Michelle, my boyfriend, Grandma, roommate, and maybe a cop are all dead because of me. Oh, and you could be next?"

She almost laughed at her imagined reaction from him. She glanced again. He was very athletic and beautifully built but could he handle even being her protection? Umm, no she was the protector in this instance. And Michelle decided that she would not tell and that was the best protection she could offer him.

Her thoughts were jarred by her phone vibrating it was Ms.E from the Cruise and the one by the old job.

Ms. E: "Hey Rocky," [spellcheck] Michelle laughed, "we are having a Fireside chat at our church tonight just a little Bible study would you like to come? I have no one else to invite. Bring your little friend too."

Michelle thought for a moment and then quickly responded before she changed her mind and replied, "Yes Ma'am I would love it, I really need it thank you so much for thinking of me."

Rocki really meant that she needed to calm her nerves and she knew that going to church and having a certain sort of feeling like Grandma E was there with her is what she needed. She wasn't so sure about Michael. She had the feeling he didn't have the same love for church as her. The way he escaped on the cruise before Ms. E started to pray and even when she said grace over the food, let her know he knew enough to know who God was but didn't want anything to do with that.

"Everybody didn't jump in feet-first like Mario," Michele thought.

"Time," as that janitor said. She stole another glance at Micheal who was looking dead at her, she did a little wave. And gestured for him to check his phone. She forwarded the text from Ms.E and chuckled as she watched Michael try his best not to hide his disgust.

But he texted back, "Sure let's do it." At the same time, Michael received a text that read, "Was it her?"

The text came in Michael looking down in disgust responded nope, I'll look into more leads and was about to put his phone on Do not disturb until Michelle gestured for him to respond. As he was responding to another text from "The Client." "Okay, time is on our side for now."

The fireside Bible study was a cozy setting of sofas, beanbags chairs set up to some in disorder, but it was warm and inviting. The lights were dim; bright enough to read and see everyone but dim enough to feel comfortable to talk. The only thing that made Rocki feel uncomfortable was she had a big ol' Living room bible as one person called it and everyone had downloaded a Bible app on their phone. She wasn't out of touch, she just never felt the need for it before. She downloaded it but still chose to read from Grandma E's Bible.

Pastor J was what you would call a gentle giant towering ,booming yet friendly voice; authoritative, yet somehow gentle, concerning, and warm. Michael was all too familiar with that kind of voice so he decided to hang back on one of the further seats and observe. Whereas Rocki went all the way to the front with Ms.E. She looked back helplessly as she was ushered up to the front. Michael mouthed "teacher's pet" and she stuck out her tongue to Michael. The music was at a mild calming volume just loud enough to hear and low enough to converse.

"Today we will be reading and analyzing Isaiah 55:6-7. Seek ye the Lord while he may be found, call ye upon him while he may be near" Pastor J finished reading and looked around, for effect, Michael thought. He braced himself for the brainwashing to begin.

"Now what are your thoughts on this or what this means to you?" Michael sat up at this, he had never in his whole life heard this in his dad's church. Have an opinion? the Bible is based on facts, how can someone tell how he feels about it? Michael's mind raced and he wondered why this affected him so much.

"Okay, no one has an opinion? Many may miss the awesomeness of God, His blessings, and his promises…"

"So you're saying God is going to just leave us stranded one day?" Michael interrupted, shocking himself. He was surprised and ashamed as everyone's eyes were on him.

Another person raised his hand, "I don't think it's that extreme," another person countered.

Pastor J again was quiet, he stared around for effect, again Michael thought .Then he said with a smile, will there come a time when we will cry out to God and his mercy will have run out? God is saying He wants us to turn away from sin and come back to him before we no longer can keep sinning and running back to Him. I know some of you are saying that it's not that easy. God knows every person's measure of faith and heart, the righteous man has been given the ability and grace to continuously reach out to God and grow in Him. We have to invite Christ into our hearts and live a life pleasing to Him that's righteous living. He expects us to willingly let Him rule over our lives, knowing that He is over all this," gesturing with his hands stretched far apart.

A young man sitting beside Michelle meekly raised his hands, "Yes Diego?" Pastor J responded, "It's an open forum, ask away." "How can we invite God in?" Diego asked.

Pastor J said "I'm glad you asked, and this is for all of you in attendance (EVEN YOU). I invite you to receive the Lord Jesus Christ into your life. If you would repeat after me, Dear Lord Jesus Christ I am a sinner. I know you have died on the cross to save me from my sins I open my heart to receive you Please forgive me for all of my sins. Direct me from this day and I will serve you in all I say, think, or do. Now if you said this prayer and meant it with your heart you are now saved and know that we are here to help you on this new journey. Walk in this Salvation knowing you are a part of God's Kingdom. And with that, I think that is the perfect way to end today's Bible Session. Next week, we will go more in-depth on the

Scripture and also I need your help in a matter and only you all can help me with this."

"Aha," Michael thought, "I knew he was too good to be true, where there is smoke there is always fire. I almost thought he was different." He knew it Michael was almost skipping as they were leaving. Michelle took it for his excitement of becoming "Saved". He tried to calm down because he could tell she was ready when Pastor J to join if he hadn't swept her away when he did. He decided she was going to find out on her own but he wanted to have a little study of his own with her. Make her see the real light. They made their way to his house. He thought she wouldn't be able to escape easily when he had to break it to her. So he made a last-minute ruse of wanting to prepare her dinner.

Dinner consisted of chicken, waffles, and a salad. It would've been ok had it all not been frozen and leftover. Michelle didn't mind, in fact, she thought it was cute. It seemed like he just swanted to spend more time with her. The vibe of the evening was beautiful for lack of a better word. He pulled out an old record.

Michelle was surprised they even made them anymore and said as much.

Michael looked at her feigning surprise "You didn't know this ages just like fine wine."

Michael pulled out his choice of album. "Patrice Rushen, or," Pulling out another one "Donna Summers is honestly all I have."

"What?" Michelle turned to him feigning surprise. "I thought that record players were for people who only listened to Nat King Cole or Frank Sinatra and smoked cigars."

"No, we are the ones they don't talk about. The ones that drink beer and listen to songs on the other side." Michael joked.

He chose Patrice Rushen and poured two glasses of scotch and gestured for Michelle to join him in the living room. She drank a little too fast she surmised after feeling the room spin within minutes of drinking. She decided to drink no more. She didn't know she and Michael both had the same feeling. He glanced at the bottle.

"what's wrong?" Michelle inquired.

"I've never had such a fast reaction to my drink before It's not bad, like how can it go bad? I've only had it for one year." He set the bottle to the side as the album played in the background. Michael grabbed her up to dance as she looked like she was lost in thought.

"Come back Michelle, where do you go? Like today when that news was breaking on the screen you had such grief on your face." He felt her body harden.

"Relax," Michael said voice a little slurry, "You're safe with me I will never let anyone harm you."

Michelle looked into his eyes and believed every word he was saying. They began to dance together in that unspoken agreement and both stumbled but not from the liqueur but from the briefcase Michael always was carrying around. He picked up a briefcase and slung it across the room between the bathroom and bedroom wall. Michelle laughed "Your stuff fell out," Michael looked and said "I'll get it later right now I have other stuff to attend to," and with that, he kissed her. Not no kiss as if to hurry to the sex part but a skyrocket into orbit kiss. Michelle felt as if her soul was wrapped in that kiss. She opened her eyes and peered straight into Michael's eyes, his soul. She was excited, scared, and loved all in one.

Her hands found his shirt and started to unbutton it when he grabbed both her hands and said, "Are you sure?" she kissed his hands this time and he released her hands and she continued her journey first his shirt then his pants. She looked down to see he himself was just as excited. She rescued him by releasing him from his boxers and pushed him onto the couch to undress. Her mind was in a mixture of shock and excitement at her courage and also this would be her first time with consent. She was fine but she kept having too many flashes coming in her head, from Mario to her grandmother to Ms. E, Pastor J, and even Mr.Des She shook her head again to erase all those images and focused on the task at hand. She straddled Michael he moaned as she positioned his love in him. He looked as if he was half out of it but he opened his eyes and grasped her by the waist as he made his introduction. Michelle matched his moans and with each thrust, the room became darker and darker just as they both were drifting off, Michelle and Michael both felt a release.

It was sometime much later when Michelle awakened it was still dark she look over at her phone it was 4:45 am. She got up and realized she had slept slumped over on the couch. Micheal moved a little under her still very much asleep. Michelle stood up and grabbed her clothes and went to take a shower. She felt a little embarrassed partially because she couldn't remember the night's event but the throbbing of her "box" made her aware of a least a portion of the night's festivities. She smiled at the thought as she finished showering and got dressed. She felt, trying to find a word as she made her way into the living room She watched as Michael slept without care. And she felt... safe was all she could come up with and that's all that was needed. She was watching Michael so intently she didn't remember to step over the mess Michael made earlier. She stooped down to clean up the mess and that's when she saw first a picture of her when she was stripping and then an old ID from when she was in college as Michelle. She looked up at him confused and hurt. Then fear took over, she felt he knew earlier when she first saw the broadcast. Her Grandma always says where there is smoke there is fire. She became angry as tears fell heavily . Who was he why was he chasing her , She watched him sleep and decided against the urge to take the knife that seemed to be calling her from the kitchen counter and plunge it into his neck. She did however take the pics and tape them all around the room in the bathroom. She heard him stirring and decided it was time to leave .Knowing if he awoke he would easily overpower her.She grabbed everything that belonged to her and made her exit.

She ran to the elevator just as she heard the ding to alert her someone was coming up but decided against using the elevator in case he woke up and she was still waiting at the elevator. She took the steps two at a time. Flagged down a cab and made it home in record time. She decided to get some stuff and lay low at a hotel until she could figure something out. She felt, for the first time in a long time... Unsafe.

Michael scratched his head wondering how a little thing like Scotch could leave him so disoriented, He popped up as the answer came to him. The Client! But how?! He felt in his bones that the text received was too nonchalant for his taste he called out to Michelle but there was no response. He looked over at his phone, it read 5:12 am. He thought maybe she was embarrassed he slowly was starting to piece together a little bit of last night's events.

He knew part of the events from his state of undress and his manhood covered in her dew, that lovemaking happened. He was angry that he couldn't remember. He thought I'll just act as though I remembered, he chuckled a mischievous plan came to mind, he removed his sock the only thing he had left on, and planned to join her in the shower. As he got closer he didn't hear any water running, he opened the door and that's when he saw that all the contents of his briefcase were taped all over the bathroom.His heart leaped into his throat wait, Rocki?! Had The Client kidnapped Michelle? Here he had promised to take care of her. He ran to get the phone. He frantically dialed her number but it went straight to voicemail.

"Rocki I'm so sorry I promise Im going to do what's right I promise. Please please answer the phone. You are safe I promise." He hung up and ran to put on some more clothes. He stopped and looked up in the air, and mockingly screeched. "She believed in you and you let this happen?" At the same time, Michael police force instincts kicked in and he noticed the door was open and he soon realized that he wasn't alone, just as he felt the blade across his neck. Michael mumbled, "I'm sorry." The Client retorted "Time's up."

   ... The Client watched the brief interchange between Michelle and Michael on the newsroom floor. Jealousy rose as Michelle and Michael playfully flirted with each other. The Client almost savored the fact that both would be dead by tonight. The job at the newsroom was easy, just a lowly janitor that no one noticed at all. Some would be offended but it gave The Client the perfect assignment. The Client thought it may be worth keeping to make extra money because after Rocki, Michelle, or whatever she wanted to call herself is dead; The Client could now live and feel free. No one would understand, even if The Client verbally stated the hate harbored for Michelle. The family was torn apart, and life on the run. Tortured because of the measure that Michelle had created that The Client could never live up to. Never saw a happy ending in sight. But now The Client felt it was in view. But every killer has a limit and church was one. And The Client dared not step inside as Michelle and Michael made their way in.

"Just wait." The Client had to keep saying over and over; salivating at the impending doom that awaited Michelle. They were almost skipping on the way out. And The Client was almost skipping too. Because the plan was to kill Michael and then to kill Michelle at her house. Because of Michael's strength and training, The Client knew they were no match for Michael but because of his love for Scotch, which the Client knew from research, The Client watched as Michael left that morning, snuck up to his apartment, and laced his Scotch.

If it turned out it wasn't Michelle then Michael was not needed and therefore his assignment was up. But the reaction that was shown as they both watched the News Segment told The Client all that was needed to know that was in fact, Michelle.

The Client was almost salivating being that close to Michelle unrecognizably. If The Client wasn't so afraid of being caged in, Michelle would have lost her life right on the newsroom floor. But, the advantage of time was in The Client's grasp. So The Client pulled the seat back in the car and snuggled in to wait. The siren of a passing ambulance startled The Client and looking at the phone's loud blare of 4:30, the Client had fallen asleep and now in a panic time was slipping away because daylight would be approaching soon. The Client reached into the back seat and pulled out a thin small scalpel and made the way up the elevator.

As the Client was exiting the elevator, someone was going down the stairs. It was kind of odd that they hadn't chosen the elevator but maybe it was some eco-friendly, bourgeois, coffee guzzler. decided to take the stairs to get their "steps in". But as The Client stealthily made treks towards Michael's door and noticed it was open. The floor creaked as The Client crossed the threshold and saw Micheal at attention. Not bad, thought The Client. Michael was pretty much out of it but The Client didn't know if they should wait until Michelle came out of the bathroom or just kill him now. But then decided on pulling Michelle out of the shower to watch as The Client slit him from ear to ear, and then explain everything to Michelle before The Client took Michelle's life.

But going into the bathroom first thing The Client saw were the pictures taped everywhere. The Client was confused, angry, and a little dazed. Michelle knew who he was. How long had it been since she was gone? Had they argued? Not from the way his soldier was on display; the night looked like it went pretty well. The person leaving may have been Michelle. The

Client went back to finish Michael when he began to stir. The hallway closet which had been the only place of solace growing up was now where The Client ran to. And watched as Michael was frantically running around and calling Michelle. Anger coursed throughout The Client at the pain and anguish in Michael's voice at the thought of losing Michelle. Something noone had ever felt for The Client, and like a tiger, The Client sprang into action. And with two words, "times up," ended Michael's suffering.

Michelle was in a whirlwind, she replayed the voicemail over and over again. Michael sounded so sincere. She stayed at the hotel but didn't know if she should go to work. She was tired of running. She would confront Michael and also plead if he had any feelings for her to tell her everything he knew and why he was looking to end her life. She sat and thought about the situation. Was it time to bring in the cops and get them to help her? If Michael knew all along and the pictures show he had, maybe he had become an ally. She had to believe no weapon formed against her was going to prosper.

She shook her head at that. She just sinned by having sex, was God even protecting her? She had to get back right, she started praying asking God to forgive her.

"I don't even remember it. Does it even count." Wait had he drugged her? Was he going to kill her last night? But he was drunk too. No, it was just a strong liqueur. She took another shower this time scrubbing hard. The more she thought the harder she scrubbed as if to show God she was erasing all the sin. As she rinsed she replayed the voicemail in her mind. "Let me make it right." He was almost begging. She still had to be cautious, but she had to believe he would help. Just as she was getting dressed her phone rang again. This time it was Ms. E. She hurriedly picked up, she needed her strength. But Ms. E's voice on the other end did not convey strength, just the opposite. "Michelle I'm so sorry I didn't have anyone else to call. I fell, can you come help me, please." Ms. E scraped out.

"Of course what is your address? She wrote down the address and called her office. Sara answered which was odd because Michael took the calls before coming out on the news floor around 11:00.

"Sara, I have an emergency I won't be in."

Sara chuckled "Real funny you and Michael both have emergencies, did y'all run off and get married? I got his email this morning an hour ago that he had to tend to a family emergency and would keep me abreast as soon as he could."

Michelle just sat looking at the phone in a daze but had no time to really take it all in. She assured Sara she would only be absent for the day. As she made her way to Ms. E's house she couldn't help but think about Michael. Had he gone to go make it right ? Or he realized that he was found out and was somewhere licking his wounds until they die down. She arrived at Ms. E's house and was met with the ambulance who she called on the way she parked her car in the driveway and got into the ambulance and held Ms. E's hand as the ambulance made its way to the hospital.

Ms. E was going to be alright she had sprained her hip and right arm from the fall but she could leave with strict instructions to rest. After much persuasion from Ms.E ,Michelle agreed to stay with her and help her heal. This also gave Michelle time to figure out her next move; she decided she couldn't go back to work and she changed her number so no one could have any access to her, what if Michael had relayed everything to her? She couldn't take any chances.

Taking care of Ms. E was such an easy task. Michelle sometimes felt guilty. She didn't tell her the whole truth. She explained that she was let go because of budget cuts and she would find something soon. Ms. E put in one call to Pastor Draehs and voila, Michelle had a job working in the church office.

Days turned into weeks and then months and a half and Michelle felt the defensive walls coming down once again. When she wasn't watching Ms. E she had taken a class to get her gun license and also self-defense classes once Ms. E could manage on her own. Ms. E talked Michelle into staying longer and Michelle didn't know who was more excited at the idea, her or

Ms. E. She hadn't felt this free since she was back home and a kid. Although she worked. For 4 days at the church she would volunteer for the food drive and to help the elderly. Her time was so consumed she had

forgotten all about Michael and the evil that followed her, sometimes. But she had become stronger in Faith and her fear was becoming more distant as she grew in her faith. She found out she loved working in the nursery even though that meant missing Service and watching it later because she was with the kids. This Sunday she determined to be in Service because a guest preacher was coming and Pastor J wanted everyone in attendance in one Service.

Michelle couldn't explain it but she was excited when Sunday came. She almost didn't make it because she became very sick the night before and had a pain in her right side that had been coming and going for some weeks now. She made a mental note to make a doctor's appointment if she didn't feel better by tomorrow. She and Ms. E did their own Bible Study and last night it talked about the weapon being formed but it wouldn't prosper. Michelle opened up to Ms. E about almost everything; including the loss of her first love but she left out that the killer was after her or that she was even being looked for. She told only about how much Grandma E and Ms. E reminded Michelle so much of each other and how she always had her in church. Ms. E just paused as if she saw into her soul. "One day then you'll tell me how a beautiful, smart, church-going woman ended up in the strip club down the street. Time will tell you when you can release it all. Give it to God for now. The testimony will come later, baby, okay?"

"Yes ma'am," Michelle stammered. and Ms. E left it at that now demanding her tea. All night she tossed and turn at the simple thought of giving it to God and speaking her truth. She believed that is why she became so nauseous. But today she decided to give it to God and already felt some of her past fears dissipating.

She and Ms. E made their way to the church house and Ms. E, although completely recovered, would use the wheelchair to navigate to the front of the church for better seats. Michelle would wheel her to the front and then go sit in the back. Today the air was charged in anticipation of this visiting Preacher. The Choir was so amped up it felt as if the angels themselves were

singing. Michelle closed her eyes to take it all in as the Pastor got up to pray. His voice while booming was so soothing Michelle felt something wash over her she looked around to see if anyone else felt how she felt. She stood not of her volition as tears poured down her face as the Pastor spoke to God to forgive and for us to let go of everything holding us down.

Michelle wanted to wait until the preacher spoke to go to the altar but the voice of her Pastor, the last words of encouragement from Ms.E, and the longing in her heart for God caused her to move toward the altar people started clapping and praising and she knew it was for her. She felt Grandma E and kept walking.

The arrival of the visiting Pastor broke her attention. She didn't want to shake away this feeling that was playing before her but the visiting Pastor looked exactly like.... Mario?! She didn't realize she was running towards the altar now but she didn't know if she was running to the Salvation God had witheld for her or to make her way to her love ? Her mind was racing with so many questions and then He glanced her way, recognized her but then shock and horror set in as he looked beyond her horrified.Michelle turned in the direction he was looking and was facing the barrel of a gun and those eyes...

The Client couldn't take it anymore, she lost track of her, she stopped coming to work, and was no longer at her apartment. But then as luck would have it The Client saw her wheeling some old lady out a clinic a couple days ago, and followed her to some beautiful house on the outskirts of town. What angered The Client more was that Michelle escaped again. Sunday came and The Client paced back and forth in front of the church, scared to enter but kept talking until it felt like the anger would explode. The Client walked and saw Michelle going towards the front and she became incensed at the thought that now she was about to make it God. She yelled her name but Michelle was so caught up she didnt hear and then The Client looked up and saw a much older Mario. She shook her head and was like, "No I killed

him." She pulled the hoodie off her head and in a daze she watched Mario run towards Michelle. The screams of the parishioners brought her out of her daze. Michelle turned and looked at The Client. This time with the Hoodie off and really looked at her...

Michelle looked to what caused the horror to wash over Mario and came Face to face with ... wait, Santori?!She said her name to reason with her and got out, "Santori, no!" She saw the gun, she heard the bang and turned to run back to Mario, to safety, sure that he was an angel coming to take her home she felt the bullets rip through her and as she fell, she was consumed in darkness and felt an overwhelming sense of peace? She surrendered to the darkness enveloping her and the unborn child she had yet to discover ....

Santori watched in glee as Michelle dropped and then Mario ran from the Pulpit and covered Michelle. To Santori it was almost like an angel covering her.Oh well , maybe he didn't die before but she wasn't going to make that mistake again?She raised her gun, but her glee was only for a moment, as she heard the sirens, she tucked the gun in her hoodie and ran once again to the exit and out the door to freedom; she exhaled and waited for the peace she fantasized and wished for all her life to finally wash over her ...

Epilogue

Satori ran as if her life depended on it. She always said the people who ran after killing someone were cowards but here she was running. She realized she would never get the freedom she now had behind bars. She had parked the car two blocks away and just made it inside as the police and fire trucks came wailing past. She thought to herself. "See I made it safely ,things already looking up."

All the pain her father bestowed upon her because of Michelle. The late-night and early-morning beatings. How he said he wished he would have left her with her real mother who Satori never met. How she spent her whole life trying to be somebody else for her dad. She watched as Michelle jabbed him in the eye with the pencil instead of just laying there as she

had on many nights. One act ruined all their lives. And yet Satori still didnt feel what she needed to feel.

She knew there was only one thing left to do. A final end to her pain and suffering. It hit her as she made her way to the one person who would leave her feeling that this was all justified ...

Part Two: "Justification" THE DUOLOGY coming soon.